STRANDED

(SPACE OUTLAW 2)

DOMINIQUE MONDESIR

Stranded
(Space Outlaw Book 2)

www.Dominiquemondesir.com

Cover art by info@dominicwalsh.com

Edited by Andrea Harding

1

The lights on the bridge had gone out. Sirens wailed and screeched. Red flashing lights highlighted dangers on multiple levels. The eerie red glow they cast over Saoirse's face didn't inspire much hope in Phoenix.

"What have we got?" Phoenix shouted over the sirens.

Saoirse's reply was inaudible.

"What?"

"It doesn't look good! The engine readings are off the charts. Shields are down--" The words were snatched out of Saoirse's mouth as the ship launched everyone off their feet. Saoirse wiped blood from her forehead before dragging herself back to the ship's controls. "Because of the lack of power, we don't have any shields to protect us from this asteroid field. If we don't land soon we will be ripped apart!"

"I'm too young to die," Plowstow cried.

"Can we make it to the planet?" Phoenix asked.

"Make it, yes. Land safely, no," said Saoirse.

"Fucking wonderful. Just fucking wonderful! I have been on a total of three spaceship rides, and two of them have crash-landed." Phoenix stabbed a button next to the wall beside him, turning on the ship's coms. "L, how's engineering looking?"

Phoenix could feel a ball of tension growing in his stomach as he received nothing but static on the other end of the line.

"L--"

"I heard you the first time!" L's voice crackled through the system.

"Well..."

"How do you think it's going? I'm ankle deep in oil and ship coolant. I don't know how this heap of junk is staying aloft."

"Well, that's reassuring," said Phoenix.

"We're nearing the planet's atmosphere. How much time can she give us?" Saoirse asked.

"L, Saoirse wants to know how much time--" Another unseen object slammed against the ship, and Phoenix grabbed the wall to steady himself. "L! Saoirse wants to know how much time we have!"

Static answered Phoenix's question. He looked over to Saoirse, whose face had paled.

"L!"

"Phoenix...we...are..." The words came scattered through the static, like a flock of pigeons trying to take flight.

"We are what, L?"

"We're going down," she said.

The force of the ship entering the atmosphere threatened to tear off the ship's outer hull, as well as Phoenix's own skin. "I can't believe this shit is happening again!" said Phoenix.

"At least you have a seat this time," said Saoirse.

"Funny." Phoenix gripped the armrest of his chair, his fingers digging into the material.

Knuckles turned white. Heads pressed flat against seats.

The ship bucked like a bull at a rodeo, wanting to veer off course. It jerked right to left, left to right, unsure what direction it wanted to head in, trying to find a way out of its misery.

Phoenix gritted his teeth as he felt the force of the Gs pull against his skin. His stomach lurched, threatening to spill its contents from both ends. Smoke billowed from one of the main consoles, and Phoenix brought his foot up to stomp out the small fire.

"Whose idea was it to come here, anyway?" Plowstow asked.

"Saoirse, can you make the landing?" Phoenix asked, ignoring Plowstow.

"I can--" Saoirse jerked the flight controls and the ship made a hard left. Sweat and blood coated her brow. She stared at the viewing panel in front of her. Jaw set firm, she appeared to be having a battle with the ship itself–willing it to stay on course, keeping it there with nothing but sheer willpower and stubbornness. "I can try," she finally replied.

"We ain't gonna make--"

"Plowstow! Shut up!"

Phoenix leaned forward in his chair, pressing the button that enabled him to communicate with the whole ship.

"Everyone listen up! This is your captain speaking."

Saoirse raised one eyebrow as she gave Phoenix a sideways look.

"I always wanted to say that. Anyway... We are going to be landing shortly, on this beautiful home planet of L's. I want everyone to brace themselves. Make sure all objects are safely secured and tucked away. On behalf of me and my crew, I would like--"

"Phoenix!" Saoirse and Plowstow both yelled.

Phoenix looked toward the viewing screen and his breath was snatched from his lungs. There was nothing but brown as far as the eye could see. It was everywhere–rolling hills and mountains of the stuff.

No other feature dominated the planet so much. There was no green. There was no blue. There was nothing in between. It was just brown.

Phoenix realised something almost too late. The brown mass was getting larger and larger by the second. It was coming at them fast. Too fast.

"Saoirse!"

"Working on it."

As Saoirse pulled and jerked the controls to and fro, anyone with half an eye could see it was a losing battle. There was nothing she could do.

The ship's nose pointed downwards, and everyone grabbed hold of whatever they could, beginning to lift from their seats. The descent was too fast, too uncontrollable.

As flames danced along the metal nose the ship twisted and turned, speeding towards the scenery below.

Phoenix could see it coming, and there wasn't a thing in the world that he could do. "Brown. Shit!"

2

The ship hit the sand like a stone skimmed across a lake. It skipped and bounced, leaving bits of metal and debris in its wake. Finally coming to a stop, it rested peacefully against the brown sand, dead and silent.

Phoenix opened his eyes to survey the scene around him. Chaos. Metal paneling hung from the ceiling of the ship. Exposed wires still sparked and flared as the last remaining current escaped from their clutches.

"Is everyone--" Phoenix wiped the sweat that coated his face, swallowed the lump that was in his throat and tried again. "Shit. Is everyone okay?"

"Are we alive?" said Plowstow.

"Seem to be, Plowstow. I would hate to think that I died and you came into the afterlife with me."

Plowstow checked himself over religiously, tutting at a cut here and a mark there. He shook his head sadly as his gaze landed on a tear in a jacket that he had found on the ship, and he uttered a soulful groan. "Will you look at this! Just found this, I have. Argh! It's ruined now."

"Saoirse, all good?" asked Phoenix.

Saoirse unclipped herself from her chair and got up. "I'm going to check on L," she said, leaving the bridge without a backwards glance.

"I take it we landed?" Freyan popped his head through the door.

"Yes, Doc. It happens we have. I would ask how the landing treated you, but you appear to be fine."

"Well, you know how strong and durable the Bloodless are, my good fellow. It would take more than a mere crash to injure me."

"So it wasn't your cries of terror I heard earlier?" said Plowstow.

"Phoenix, will I be needed for anything before we depart?" Freyan asked, ignoring the question.

"No. Just make sure you have all the medical supplies that you need and anything else that could be useful to you. I doubt we will be coming back to this ship."

Freyan gave him a nod before slipping back into the bowels of the ship.

Phoenix unstrapped himself and cast a look around the bridge. There was nothing worth saving. Everything was either burnt or simply didn't work anymore.

"Plowstow, get your shit and meet me outside."

Phoenix collected the few items he had brought with him from home and made his way toward the back of the ship, where the ramp was located. Or where it *should* have been located. The whole section of the back of the ship was now missing.

Phoenix walked towards it open-mouthed. How they had managed to land this ship, in the state that it was in, was beyond him. But then again, with Saoirse at the helm, maybe it wasn't just a lucky break after all.

He walked through the newly formed doorway and was

met by a blast of heat and humidity that stole his breath. He felt as though he had just walked into a sauna. Heat prickled his skin and the glare of the sun overhead forced him to squint.

Ahead of him, he could see the trail of parts the ship had tossed like clothes from two lovers on a one-night stand.

Phoenix turned his head left and then right. Both directions offered him the same view: an endless sea of brown sand. Nothing stirred around him, and the silence was peaceful, haunting and deadly all in one.

Freyan and Plowstow took up the spaces on either side of him, and Phoenix still remained silent. He closed his eyes, and a slow smile crept across his face. This was the first planet he had set foot on other than Earth. Digging his feet further into the sand, he allowed it to cover his shoes. He, Phoenix Jones, was now a space explorer. Bending down, he picked up the scorching hot sand in his hands. He threw one handful in the air and poured the other inside a little clear bottle.

His smile turned into a chuckle and grew into a belly laugh; Phoenix did a dance on the spot. He was on another planet! The troublemaker at school, voted most likely to end up in prison before he turned thirty... Well, he *had* been in prison, but he had been older than thirty–and technically it wasn't a prison on Earth–so that didn't count.

Running footsteps bounded behind him, and he felt the weight of someone leaping on his back. Arms wrapped around his throat and legs wrapped themselves round his stomach, and he steadied himself so he didn't topple over.

"Welcome to my home!" L said from Phoenix's back.

3

"What is this?" said Holger.

"I...I...I don't know what you mean, my lord," stuttered one of Holger's servants.

Holger's cheeks flushed red as he brushed a hand forcefully through his hair. "The question was a simple one. I fail to see how you do not understand. I didn't know I asked you such a complex question. Let us try again, shall we? What is this in front of me?"

"It's... It's...what you requested. The meal from the planet known as Earth. I believe it's called ice-cream. I--"

"Good. Good. We are getting somewhere. But this isn't what I--"

"My lord, I assure--"

The slap that Holger delivered to the female servant's face appeared weak but it still left a mark. "Do not interrupt me again."

The servant lowered her head and tried to keep her tears in check. The room was occupied by other members of Holger's staff, but they busied themselves, heads down, trying to avoid their master's wrath.

"I know this is ice-cream, but what flavour?"

The female servant looked up at Holger with wide tear-rimmed eyes. Her bottom lip trembled as she muttered something inaudible.

"I didn't quite catch that," Holger said, cupping his hand around his ear.

"I believe the humans call it vanilla."

"Ah, vanilla. That explains it, then. So this isn't chocolate?"

"I--"

"Of course it's not, because chocolate is a different colour!" Holger grabbed the bowl from in front of him and pushed the contents of the bowl in the servant's face. Twisting his hand back and forth, he made sure the contents covered her face.

"Maybe that should help you to tell the difference between the two, now that it is a bit closer to your face! Now, serve me what I asked for."

The servant stood still, too scared to move. Her gaze swept around the room and she trembled as she looked for anyone to help her, but no help came. Tears started to clean a path down her cheeks. She started to speak but it came out in a jumbled mess.

"Speak clearly," said Holger.

"We... We...don't have any chocolate, my lord."

"What do you mean?"

"The food stocks... There must have been some misunderstanding. There must have--"

"How is that person related to you?" Holger asked, pointing to an elderly servant in the distance.

"That is my mother."

"Good." Holger took out a plasma gun and shot the elderly servant in the foot. The scream that escaped her mouth froze everyone's actions.

Writhing on the floor in agony, the mother clawed at her foot as a bear would if it were caught in a trap.

The servant in front of Holger began to move but was stopped in her tracks as Holger fired near her feet.

"Where do you think you're going?"

"My lord. I... My mother--"

"Is of no concern to me. Now, what are you going to do about my meal?"

The servant shook in front of Holger. Her gaze swept to her mother, bleeding on the floor, and moved back to Holger. "I will find you what you asked for, my lord."

Alerted by a beeping, Holger glanced down at his waist, where a light blinked on and off. A frown descended over his features and he tutted loudly before addressing the room.

"Everyone out! You," he said, pointing to the servant in front of him, "get me the correct meal before the hour is up or there shall be dire consequences. And someone get that weeping bloody mess out of my sight." Holger waved his hand dismissively at the servant on the floor.

Holger rushed towards a military jacket such as his men wore, as an incoming call beeped on his wrist. It was tighter than he would have liked when he slipped it on. He tried to button it up but failed to do so. Leaving it open, he made his way towards his chair.

At a press of a button, an image appeared in front of him.

"Ah, Rustem, how good it is to see you."

A face that could pass for any human male's appeared

on a hologram in front of Holger. It was impossible to guess his age because of his dark features. Braided hair descended down his shoulders with golden bells attached to the ends.

"Holger."

Holger's face twitched slightly as he applied a greasy smile to his face. "Only my friends call me Holger. People who work for me call me 'my lord,' or 'sir.'"

"I tend to kill the people I work for," said Rustem.

"Are you threatening me? Do you know who my--"

"I am well aware whose loins you come from, Holger. As you are well aware of who I am. Let us begin this relationship on equal footing. As friends who share knowledge and wealth. Wouldn't that be better for us all?"

"Better?"

"Yes, better," said Rustem. "I was thinking nice words would be better than threats. Working towards a shared goal is always better than against each other. So let us work together, Holger."

Holger cleared his throat and brushed the jacket's sleeve with the back of his hand. "Well, Rustem, *my friend,* what have you found out?"

"Oh, a great many things. For instance, did you know that humans blink their eyes so many times in a day that it equates to having their eyes closed for thirty minutes? For a period of the day they are walking around blind. Unconscious of the world around them. How strange is that?" said Rustem.

"I mean did you find anything about Phoenix!"

"Oh, that. Why didn't you say so? Well, I have been informed that he is now in charge of a crew. It seems the Earth man acquired some friends while he was in Dredar. I have spies located on each of his crew's home-worlds, and if they land there, I will be informed."

"Good. Good. Listen, nobody can know about this. It can't be traced back to me, you hear? Father is already not taking my calls. Can you believe that I'm his one and only remaining son, and he refuses to have anything to do with me? He's always been the same, ever since I can remember. Just because of what happened on Dredar and Earth... It was hardly *my* fault, was it? I would have thought what happened to... I mean--"

"What *did* happen? I have heard rumours about it, but no one seems to want to tell me the full story. Like a virgin on the first night she is bedded, everyone skirts round the dirty naked truth," said Rustem.

"It is none of your business, and it would do you well to focus on the job I have assigned you," said Holger.

"The job is all but done, my friend."

"Make sure that it is."

"Oh, before I go," Rustem said, snapping his fingers. "There was this amazing food that the Earth people almost worship. What was it called again, err, ice-cream I think it was."

How does he know? It can't be. It must be a coincidence.

Rustem brought a bowl towards his face and picked up a spoon, lifting a mouthful towards his mouth.

"I believe they call this flavour chocolate. Truly amazing." With that, Rustem ended the call and allowed Holger to ponder the choices that he had made in life.

4

The infighting started before Phoenix knew what hit him. It all began with a simple question from Plowstow.

"Can you make her fly again?"

"Not unless you have an engine in your pocket, green man," L replied.

"Then how the hell are we going to get anywhere? I thought it was your job to look after the engine and make sure that the ship was flying okay." Plowstow stabbed a finger at the now lifeless ship and continued. "Great job you did--"

"Don't you dare have a go at her!" Saoirse said, walking towards Plowstow.

"Who am I meant to have a go at? It was her job to look after the ship. It was her job to make sure the stupid thing would stay in the air. Now we are stranded in--"

"We are not stranded. I know where we are," L muttered, her hair going dull grey.

"And where, oh where, are we?"

"Not far from the city where my brother and I stayed. All we have to do is walk," said L.

All eyes peered into the distance, taking in the heat waves bouncing off the sand. A slight humid breeze blew grains of sand up from the ground, and they all shielded their eyes. Sand dunes blocked any view of what lay beyond in the distance. If there was a city out there, it wasn't within easy walking distance.

"Walk? And how far is that?" said Plowstow.

"Not far. Maybe an hour or two."

"Argh! I can't believe this. I should never have--"

"Plowstow! No one is forcing you to come. You can always stay here and hope someone–or *something*–comes to pick you up. L, you know this area best. What do we need to do to make it to this city safely?"

"Grab any drinkable liquid, cover your head and body against the heat, and above all else, pace yourself. Moving too fast in this terrain will kill you a lot quicker than anything you encounter out there."

"Everyone do as she says. We leave in five," said Phoenix.

The sun was unbearable. It beat down upon their shoulders with the force of a bullwhip. The searing heat was relentless. Shade was nowhere to be found. This was the sun's domain, and it tortured anyone foolish enough to enter it.

Phoenix wiped the sweat from his brow and flicked it off his hand. Taking a swig of water from his bottle, he cast his gaze over the scene around him.

Sand dunes still dominated the environment. Small shrubs no more than three feet high were dotted around, their branches covered with purple needles that gave a visual warning. Large tunnel-like mounds criss-crossed the sand. The largest ones were at least two hundred feet across.

Phoenix allowed himself to slow down until he was at the back of the group, walking alongside L. Her head was lowered and her shoulders were slumped forward. Phoenix remained silent, simply sharing the peace with her.

"I didn't mean for the... I tried my best, but the stupid ship was damaged from the beginning. I couldn't have done anything to save her. She wasn't meant for such a long-haul flight. It was too much for her. I'm not saying it wasn't my fault, Phoenix. Just..." L let out a small sigh and shrugged her shoulders.

"L, I know you're sorry. It doesn't need to be said--"

"It's not that, Phoenix. I pride myself on being the best ship's engineer I can be. There isn't a problem I can't fix or an issue I can't solve. I knew that there would be problems with the ship. That there would be a chance we wouldn't make it. More than a chance, actually.

"But I wanted to take that chance. I just couldn't stop thinking about my brother; I couldn't stop thinking about how long we had been apart. Only Soul knows what trouble he could have gotten into. At any other time, I would have told you to get another ship. But I was..."

"You were blinded by the love for your family. I know how that feels," said Phoenix. He thought back over the last few months and what he had done. What he *would* have done, just to see his family again. Just to see them and make sure that they were safe. He understood.

"Look, L, if it was anyone else looking after the ship, we would be dead by now. Don't beat yourself up about it. You have given me the best thing I could ever ask for," said Phoenix.

"And what is that?"

"I'm the first human to step foot on a different planet!" Phoenix grabbed L in a bear-hug embrace, swinging her around as she giggled uncontrollably.

Unimpressed, the others stopped in their tracks and looked back at the pair. Phoenix didn't care, though; this was the adventure he had been missing for so long. He felt alive again. He felt free again. He could travel anywhere he wanted. Life wasn't restricted anymore. He had stars, planets and galaxies, that no other human had laid eyes on, to see.

His future looked bright.

5

The sun was close to setting when the crew saw lights up ahead. They blinked in and out of existence like fairy lights on a Christmas tree.

Phoenix stopped and squinted ahead. "Is that what I think it is?" he gasped.

"Yup," came the simple reply from L.

Phoenix licked his cracked, dry lips and tried to concentrate. He lifted his water bottle to his lips; a few droplets burnt on his tongue like water on hot asphalt.

"You sure those are city lights and not something else? I would hate to get lost again," said Plowstow.

"It was a few wrong turns. If you like, you can always go your own way," said Freyan.

"I was just saying, that was all."

Phoenix looked over his shoulder, puzzled, scanning the sand behind him.

L said, "Once we get to my old stomping grounds all will be forgotten. We can all have a nice hot meal, get the dirt and grime off us and just relax. Then have a few drinks.".

"Are the drinks free? Because my credit is a bit low at the moment," Plowstow grumbled.

"Yes, the drinks will be on me, Plowstow. Wouldn't want you to starve or die of thirst."

Phoenix shielded his eyes with his hand. Was that a large sand mound coming their way?

"I ain't saying I can't pay my own way, you hear? Just that life has seen me on hard times at the moment, and if one of you could see it in your hearts to show me a bit of kindness, then it won't go amiss," said Plowstow.

"Don't worry, I'm sure there are many old or disabled members of the public that you can prey on once we get to the city. Your pockets will soon be overflowing with all your ill-gotten gains," said Freyan.

"I only do what I need to do, to keep myself alive!"

Phoenix was sure of it now. Something was out there. Something was moving towards them, and it was large.

"Err...L? Are there any animals out here that could do us any harm?" asked Phoenix.

"No. Not this close to the city. Why?"

"Well there seems to be a large sand--"

"What!" L spun around and Phoenix recognised the look of fear plastered on her face. "Oh no--"

Plowstow pushed past L and took off like the hounds of hell were after him. He didn't look back. He didn't wait and see what was headed their way. He simply sprinted towards the city lights ahead of them.

"L, what's wrong?" Saoirse asked.

"It's a dust worm. Run towards the city!"

"A worm?" Phoenix said in disbelief. He turned back around and could now clearly see how big the sand mound really was–at least fifty feet across and traveling at some speed. Whatever worm created that would be able to swallow him and the rest of the crew in one bite.

"Let's move--" Phoenix turned back around, and noticed that he was the only one still standing still. "Fuckers!"

~

Phoenix's arms pumped up and down as his feet pounded the sand. The sand made a firm foothold impossible. His calves burnt and his heart punched against his chest.

Was the mound getting closer? Could he hear the shifting of the sand as the animal made its way through it like a snowplough?

Finally he caught up with the remaining members of the crew. He didn't know how long they could push this pace for; heat, sand and dry air made each lungful of breath painful. Freyan would be okay, but the heat had affected them all.

"Shouldn't we stand and fight?" said Saoirse.

"Dust worms... grow...to...two hundred...feet," L huffed.

"They grow up to two hundred feet? My gosh, I would love to have a specimen to study," Freyan said.

"They...attack...everything."

"L, save your breath," said Saoirse.

Phoenix looked up ahead and could see the distant outline of Plowstow. *Fucker hasn't even looked behind him.* He threw a sharp glance over his shoulder and couldn't quite believe what he saw. "I don't want to worry anyone, but there's more than one."

Two snake-like mounds moved almost as one, the dust worms' interest only on one thing: their next meal ahead of them.

L stumbled forward, losing her footing, and collapsed on

the sand. Saoirse went to pick her up but was pushed away by Freyan.

"I do not have muscles that tire. Save your strength."

Freyan picked up L, threw her over his shoulder, and continued running.

Saoirse and Phoenix looked at the rapidly approaching mounds and mirrored each other's worried expressions.

"Towards...city! Safe," L gasped, bouncing upon Freyan's shoulder.

"Freyan, can you run faster than you already are?" asked Phoenix.

"I can. How did you know?"

"Hunch! I want you to take L... and...get to the city!"

"But--"

"Do it!"

Freyan gave Phoenix a look that said be careful–that said they might not make it out alive. None of that mattered to Phoenix right then. He had promised to take care of L, and that was what he was going to do.

Phoenix gave Freyan a small nod and waved him forward. That was all that was needed. Freyan sprinted ahead, leaving a small dust cloud in his wake. He ran with the power of a high-performance sports car, his footing precise and sure.

As Freyan's sleek white body became smaller and smaller, a part of Phoenix wished he had asked for a ride. "Damn! Look at that boy go," he said. He looked behind once more and saw that the image was no less daunting than before. "We're nearly there."

"You don't have to reassure me, Phoenix," said Saoirse.

"Just--"

"Less talk. Run faster," she snapped.

Freyan had now passed Plowstow, and he and L made it

to the city walls first. The city loomed ahead of them like a beautiful woman now aged and down on her luck. Black smoke bellowed from her lungs as if she smoked thirty cigarettes a day. Dilapidated towers leaned at awkward angles, encased behind a stone wall.

Freyan had carried L up what appeared to be a metal ladder up the side of the city wall. Plowstow was close behind him and made his way up the ladder like a rat up a drainpipe.

Saoirse reached the ladder before Phoenix and looked behind her.

"Go! Don't wait," Phoenix yelled, waving her onward.

She cast one last look his way but didn't hesitate in making her way up the ladder.

Phoenix's breathing was pained. His legs felt like hot rubber. By all accounts, he should have already collapsed, but something kept him going. He was more of a sprinter than a long distance runner. The strides had been relatively painless until now. It seemed he was nearly out of juice.

He saw the ladder in front of him, its rusty metal offering him salvation, but his foot caught on something and he fell forward before he knew what was happening.

Rolling onto his shoulder, he came back up and reached for the first rung of the ladder. He glanced behind him and what he saw froze him on the spot.

A circular mouth with teeth as long as he was tall bore down on him. It appeared to have swallowed the sun, as he could see nothing but darkness.

6

Move, Phoenix! Fucking move!

His body didn't want to respond. It seemed frozen to the spot. A hand descended from above and snatched him up in the air. He saw ladder rung after ladder rung fly past his face in a blur.

I'd better grab one.

He reached out with both hands and grabbed whatever he could, slamming into the stone surface of the wall. His face scraped against the rock and left him with a cut lip and a black eye. He felt like his shoulders had nearly been ripped from their sockets, it had taken so much force to latch onto the ladder.

Phoenix looked below him and saw Freyan's white features staring up at him.

"Thank you for pulling me up," said Phoenix.

"I thought for a moment that I used too much force and you would forget to grab onto the ladder when the time came."

"Thank God for my survival instincts." Phoenix looked down and saw that the dust worms were circling the sand below, their bodies once again hidden under the sand. Every so often, black skin, glistening like marble, broke the surface.

"It appears that they can only detect movement on the sand," Freyan said, following his gaze.

"Lucky for us."

With one final downwards glance at the terror that lay below, Phoenix began making his way upwards. A midnight-blue hand appeared in front of his face. He grabbed it and allowed himself to be helped up onto one of the rock ledges cut into the wall at different levels all the way to the top.

L waved at him exhaustedly from where she lay in a heap on the floor. Plowstow sat with his back to the wall not much further away, chest heaving and head between his legs. Phoenix took a spot next to L and sank down, his shaking legs giving out underneath him.

"You're still alive, I see," muttered Phoenix.

"Yeah, well, you know..." L said, smiling at him.

"That was tense. I thought we had a bug problem back at home, but that takes the biscuit," said Phoenix.

"Dust worms are normally found deep out in the wild. They are rarely found this close to a city. I just don't understand. Something has changed, and not for the better," L said, pushing her hand through her yellow hair. "All cities and villages on Tingo are located on large rocks like these, the reason being they can not be attacked by dust worms. Travel from one city or village to the next is dangerous and costly."

"You've been gone a while. Things change. Sometimes not for the better," said Phoenix.

"Hmm." L got up from where she sat and dusted herself off. "Let's see by how much, shall we?"

Dust hung in the air like a thin veil, tinting the whole city brown. The buildings were old, crippled and decrepit. Boards adorned the windows of more than one building and metal shutters on others remained permanently down.

Towers dotted the skyline like spots on a teenager's face, but they too seemed to be on their last legs. As the sheet of day was slowly pulled away to allow night to take over, floating round orbs gave off what light they could. Most flickered on and off with dying effort.

Larger orbs floated hundreds of feet in the sky, never staying stationary. Their black metal gave them an ominous appearance. Phoenix stopped in his tracks to gawk at them.

"They collect energy from the sun and power drills below the desert's surface that collect water," said L, pointing to the large orbs. "But the thing is, no one in their right mind would drill so close to the city. The disturbance it causes would attract too much attention from the worms."

The crew moved through the streets as one with L leading the way. Phoenix snapped his head back and forth with a slight frown on his face. The air smelled of oil and tasted of sorrow. Laughter was nowhere to be found. Legs could be seen sticking out of doorways, and coughs bounced off alleyway walls.

"You are disappointed?" Freyan asked.

"No, I... Yes, I am. Just...I thought... I just thought that my first alien city would be more awe-inspiring, rather than reminding me of a third world country back home. I mean, where are the floating robots and mind-blowing gadgets? This is just so...depressing."

"It is good you saw this first. Not every world is advanced, although they may be able to space-travel. Some worlds have hit an economic downturn, some may have gone through civil unrest. The reasons for how they have become as they are are many. But remember this, Class One planets are best avoided. Higher-grade technology equates to better surveillance. Better surveillance means that we are easier to apprehend."

Phoenix gave a nod.

"This all looks so different," L said. "So... So...disgusting. When I first came here, years ago, everything was on the up and up. Everything was clean. Everything was nice. Now look at it." She spun on her heels, taking in everything around her.

Shouts came from their left, quickly followed by a body being thrown out of a window. Glass littered the floor and the body lay in a heap. It moaned slightly and tried to lift itself up off the ground but fell back down, face first.

Freyan moved towards the body but was stopped by Phoenix, who grabbed his arm.

"I don't know what y'all are complaining about. This is my kind of place," Plowstow said with a slight nod of his head.

"I'm not surprised," said Saoirse.

"What's not to like? Cheap drinks, cheap females to suit most races, and fights aplenty. I am going to have some fun here," said Plowstow, walking off down a side road.

"We'll be staying at an inn called Dusty's! Meet us there!" L shouted at Plowstow's retreating back.

Plowstow gave a single wave to show that he had heard and then he was gone.

7

Plowstow walked down one side street after the other, constantly looking over his shoulder. He wished he could have stayed out in the open, as the alleyways and back streets seemed busier. They teemed with life.

Food carts offered certain delicacies you wouldn't find out in the open. They offered to cure the user of certain tastes that were frowned upon in public. Drug-roasted nuts sizzled over an open flame, their aroma wafting on the breeze. The smell tickled Plowstow's nose, causing him to sneeze.

Scantily clad females waved at passersby, seemingly unaffected by the cold breeze. Plowstow gave them a longing gaze before quickly moving on. There would be time enough for that later.

He took twisting backstreet after twisting backstreet, going deeper and deeper into the city's underbelly. The further he went, the thinner the herd became, until there was nothing but the creatures that crawled from one picked-clean bone to the next. Plowstow cast his gaze from one end of the alley to the other, happy that no one was around.

He pulled back his wrist and dialled a code into his holocom.

He waited for the signal to be picked up at the other end. The beeping of his call tried to get through, and the shadows seemed to jump from one wall to the next. A sound behind him made him spin around. A body seemingly made up of rags stared at him intently. It didn't say anything, it just stared.

"Leave," said Plowstow.

But still the body remained.

Plowstow shook his head and pulled out the small sidearm strapped to his hip. He fired two shots into the body of rags, dropping it where it stood.

"What was that noise?" said a projection emitting from his wrist.

"I just had to stun someone. Nothing to worry about," said Plowstow.

"Oh. Nothing that will lead back to me, I hope?"

"It was a nobody. Now, are we still in business?" said Plowstow.

"It all depends, really--"

"Depends on what? This was a done deal, you hear? A spit and handshake sort of thing. Do you know what I had to go through to get this? I could go to any other bidder with this knowledge and they would pay double what I'm asking. This ain't some game," said Plowstow.

"Easy, easy, honey. If you had let me finish, I was simply going to ask if you had the item in question," said the hologram.

"If I didn't have it, I wouldn't be calling you, would I?"

"I guess not."

"Now, are we in business or not?" said Plowstow.

"We are, we are. But the price you are asking seems a bit steep. I was thinking about twenty-five percent less than your asking price. Times are tough--"

"No deal."

"Come now, darling. Who could you get to pay what you are asking? Be reasonable."

"The price stands."

"Well, I hope you find a good enough buyer who can afford your rate, plus give you peace of mind that the transaction will not be traced back to you. Because even if whispers of this get out..." The hologram tutted. "You will be forever watching your back. Can you trust another buyer not to utter your name under duress?"

"I don't--"

"Seeing how you have been so loyal to those you class your friends."

"Ten percent less than the asking price," said Plowstow.

"Hmm, ten percent. Ten percent... Cost of fuel, plus the inconvenience of me coming to you... How about twenty?"

"Fifteen."

"Done. Send me the location of where to meet you and this deal shall be done," said the hologram.

"I'm sending the location now. How long will you be? I hate waiting for credits that are owed to me."

"I'm getting the information now. Let me see... Oh, you're closer to me than I thought. I shall be with you in a few days."

"I didn't think you got the message I sent. Time and space on the ship was...tight. I tried my best to make it clear," said Plowstow.

"It came through fine, darling. I was surprised when I heard from you, so I knew whatever you had must be good.

Anyway, honey, I would love to catch up on old times but I gotta go. Don't miss me too much."

"Just bring me my credits," Plowstow said, signing off.

Plowstow walked past the still unconscious body on the floor and barely gave it a glance, scratching at his collar. He knew the credits were good but doubts still plagued him. Was it worth it? Was it worth risking what he had just found? What had he *actually* found? Friends he always had enough of, but credits...now credits he could always use more of.

"Fancy someone to take care of your worries?" said a smiling female in a doorway.

"You know what, I don't mind if you do," said Plowstow, walking her way.

8

Dusty's Inn was everything Phoenix imagined and more. Drunks lay on tables in what appeared to be their own vomit, the smell emitting from them mixing with the aroma of the room. The light from the ceiling overheard tried in vain to permeate the smoky den but failed miserably. The air felt thick. Alive. Phoenix waved a hand through it, clearing the space in front of him, but the smoke reclaimed its space like a jealous lover.

"Let's sit somewhere out of the way," L said, raising her voice so she could be heard.

The crew followed her lead and found a space at the back, positioned in a little alcove that offered them some privacy.

"Everyone make yourselves comfortable, I'll be back with some drinks," L said, making her way towards the bar.

Phoenix scanned the faces around them and noticed that a fair few had taken an interest in the newcomers. They stared openly in their direction, so Phoenix stared openly back.

"Well, this seems like a...*reputable* establishment," said Freyan from under a hooded cloak.

"What's with the cloak and dagger stuff?" Phoenix said, nodding Freyan's way.

"You saw how my kind were treated on the prison ship. Well, that same resentment isn't only isolated there. Ignorance relating to--" Pausing to allow a stranger to walk by, Freyan continued, "–my race, is widespread and very much alive. I had hoped that it would have disappeared, but coming to a planet like this, which isn't...as advanced as others, could lead to problems."

"Hmm, I didn't realise. Couldn't you simply alter your appearance?"

"I could but such practices are frowned upon. If caught, it would mean more trouble for us than my simply appearing as I am."

"Freyan is correct," said Saoirse. "It would be best to keep his appearance hidden while we are stationed here. This planet isn't known for its law-abiding ways. They don't have any representatives working under the Council, which means the Council's laws don't apply here."

"And what laws would those be?" asked Phoenix.

"The Council, although corrupt in so many ways, need the planets under their banner to cooperate. Law-abiding citizens are tax-paying citizens. Law-abiding citizens are easier to handle, easier to instruct, easier to--"

"Control," said Phoenix, cutting Freyan off.

"Like dumb animals," Saoirse spat.

"Yes, in so many sad ways," said Freyan. "The Council's hand is felt heavily by any person wishing to break the laws on the planets that they control. Their justice is harsh and never fair."

"Let me guess, the Council comes down on anyone that tries to better their place in life?"

"Not always, Phoenix. The one thing above all else the Council wants, needs and respects, is credit. No matter how you got it, if you are willing to spend it their way, you shall always be in their favour. But those credits hardly see their way to the poor," said Freyan.

"Rich people like to stay rich, I guess, and poor people looking for a slice of that pie doesn't sit well with them," said Phoenix.

"Which is a stupid argument to even entertain. There are enough resources around us for everyone to live comfortably," said Freyan.

"I couldn't agree with you more, Doc. But sometimes you have to take what you want by force. Sometimes life doesn't give you what you want on a platter. Sometimes life only rewards the harshest and the cruelest."

"That's a terrible way to live, Phoenix."

"That's the only way some people can live."

A noise from the bar drew all their attention towards it. A voice that they all knew too well floated on the soup-like air.

"Look, I told you I would pay for your drink!"

The response was swallowed up among the rafters.

"I don't care!"

Saoirse started to rise from her seat, but Phoenix placed a hand over her arm. She looked down at it, then back up at Phoenix with a raised eyebrow.

"You and Freyan make your way towards the front door. I won't be long."

Phoenix made a move towards the bar without waiting for a response. Saoirse could sometimes be heavy-handed where L was concerned, and right now, a heavy-handed approach was something they didn't need. Pushing past bodies, and stepping on toes so the crowded parted, Phoenix finally spotted L.

She was surrounded by three large muscle-bound males. The leader of the group had a large red Mohawk and a tattoo of what appeared to be a large worm on the side of his head.

"I told you that buying a drink is the only thing you'll get out of me. Nothing else!" said L.

The greasy smile on Mohawk's face showed that he didn't get the hint. "Come on, I ain't asking for much. Just a kiss. Just a touch. Just something to make us both feel right."

Laughter erupted from the other two and the circle grew tighter around L.

"Well, you can forget your drink then, if you're going to act like that," said L.

"Aw, I can't be having that, now, can I, boys? No drink. No touchy-touchy. Plus you did spill my drink. What am I meant to drink now?"

"You had your chance, and now it's gone," L said, blowing out her cheeks.

L tried to leave but was grabbed as she made her way past. Mohawk spun her around and began to dry hump her, while his hands tried to move under her shirt. The laughter from the other two drowned out L's protests.

Phoenix placed his hand on Mohawk's shoulder and gave it a slight squeeze. "Why don't you let my friend, here, go? Let me pay you back your drink, and we can all continue to have a nice time," Phoenix said with a smile.

"Get lost," Mohawk said, trying to shake off Phoenix's grip.

Phoenix's hand didn't move, and he squeezed a little harder. "Listen," said Mohawk, hair turning fiery red as he turned to face Phoenix. "I don't think you know who I am. Or what group I belong to. But seeing as you're new here, I'll tell you. We run this town. So I suggest that you take your fucking hand off me before I remove it."

"Anyone who says 'Don't you know who I am' isn't really someone worth knowing," said Phoenix.

"You what!"

"Turn around and walk back to your table," said Phoenix.

"I think you must be stupid. Stupid or--"

The plasma blast that blew Mohawk's leg clean off didn't silence the room. The scream that followed it had that honour.

"Now I want you to crawl back," said Phoenix.

Mohawk rolled along the floor holding the stump that used to be a leg. Blood gushed forth from it and his screams turned into whimpers.

"You think you can get away with this?" said one of Mohawk's friends, making his way towards Phoenix.

He didn't get far, as Phoenix shot him in the leg too. Mohawk's friend fell to the floor next to him, his screams of pain playing as a backing track to his leader's agony.

"You don't know what you--" Mohawk started but stopped when Phoenix placed the barrel of his plasma gun in his mouth.

"I. Don't. Care. L, let's go."

As they both made their way towards the exit, Saoirse held the door open for them.

And I thought that Saoirse was going to be too heavy-handed.

Out in the open, they saw a familiar face approach them.

"We're off to Rusty's, Plowstow," L said, leading the way.

"What! How come?"

"The clientele at Dusty's just couldn't keep their hands off the goodies," L said with a laugh.

9

The crew gathered around a table and silently sipped drinks. Rusty's was a lot quieter than Dusty's, but that wasn't really saying much in a city like this.

The level of clientele had graduated from sewage scum to pond scum. Phoenix looked around and noticed that everyone's eyes were either on their own drinks or half closed. Life seemed to have beaten any anger or hatred out of these poor souls. Now they just wanted to merely exist.

"So... Mighty fine weather we're having, this time of year," said L cheerfully. "Mighty fine indeed."

Phoenix took another sip of his drink and allowed it to warm his stomach. Whatever it was seemed to do the trick of relaxing his nerves. Maybe a little too much, he thought, pushing the mug away.

"Don't worry, Phoenix, you can relax. Drink up. Rusty's has always been quieter and more mellow than Dusty's," said L, pushing Phoenix's drink back towards him.

"What's with all the stupid names, anyway?" Phoenix asked.

"People around here lack imagination. I'm surprised my race even made it off this dustball. Everyone around here is scared of any big ideas. Scared of life. Boring. What's life without a little fun?" L said, her hair turning the colour of a sunset over crystal blue water.

"Sometimes people--"

"Are we not going to talk about the big picture here? Or are we just going to chit-chat all day?" Plowstow said, cutting Freyan off.

"What big picture would that be, Plowstow?" said Phoenix.

"Oh, I don't know. Let me think. We're stranded on this dustball of a planet without any way to get off. Without any credits to our name. With little or no supplies to keep us alive much longer."

"I'm well aware of that," said Phoenix.

"So what do *you* plan to do about it? I ain't staying on this planet a moment longer than I have to, you hear?"

"What am I going to do about it? I'll tell you what I am going to do--"

"I have a plan," said L.

As all sets of eyes turned towards her, L allowed a small smile to play across her face. She downed her drink in one and slammed her mug down on the table.

"I can get us a ship. I may be able to get us some credits."

"The act of getting these items wouldn't be illegal, would it?" said Freyan.

"No. The ship is rightfully mine, and the credits would be back-payment for a job that I did but was never paid for."

"So, this ship... Where is it?" Phoenix asked.

"Ah, that's the thing. It's being *looked after* by someone, at the moment."

"And that someone would be..." said Phoenix.

"He's called Duke. He runs a gang called the--"

"Worm Enforcers," said Plowstow.

"Another friend of yours, no doubt. Why am I not surprised?" said Freyan with a snort.

"The Worm Enforcers? What kind of shit name is that? Your planet really haven't got the whole naming thing down, have they?" said Phoenix.

"The Worm Enforcers are not to be messed with. They are vicious, backstabbing murderers, who would slit their own deliverer's throat just to make a credit," said Plowstow.

"I can see how you and they have a lot in common," said Freyan.

"Look! I may be a lot of things, but I love my old deliverer like she was the last thing in this galaxy. I would do anything for her. You hear me?"

"So what do we know about Duke?" Phoenix asked.

L and Plowstow looked at each other before either spoke.

"Well, he's..." Plowstow started.

"He can be..." L trailed off.

"He's nasty, spiteful, double-crossing, prideful," said Plowstow.

"He came through the ranks of the Worm Enforcers by violence," said L. "He kills without remorse; he is a man to be feared. He runs this whole city and has many spies."

"Plus he has a weird thing about his height," said Plowstow.

"So where is this ship, and how do we get it?" Saoirse asked.

"In the shipyard, of course," said L.

"L what are you not telling us? Phoenix asked.

"Nothing, nothing..."

"L."

"Okay. Okay. Their base of operations is in front of the shipyard. They kind of own it, but I wouldn't class what they did to get it as legal."

"How do you know the ship is even there? I mean, you have been in Dredar for a while. Anyone could have taken it," said Plowstow.

L drummed her fingers along the table before she answered. "Because I have set security measures preventing the ship being flown unless I authorize it."

"But how do you--"

"Because I am the best at what I do, Plowstow! Because I built that ship with my bare hands. It took years. But I know that ship in and out." She paused, and continued, stressing each word. "It's still here."

"So what's the plan?" asked Phoenix.

"We take back my ship, and we get my brother back," said L with fire in her voice.

10

A wet thud echoed off the walls of the warehouse. The sound was ominous but had an incessant hypnotic pattern to it.

Blake walked into the warehouse and nodded to a few of the men standing guard. He kicked the few that were asleep awake as he passed by. Bottles littered the floor, and dirty plates were piled sky high on any available surface.

Blake came to a stop and pinched a plate by two fingers. Its greasy contents slid to the floor and landed with a flop. Blake pinched the bridge of his nose, breathing in and out slowly.

It was no good.

He threw the plate at the group of men he had just woken, and it hit one square in the face.

"What the fuck, Blake?" said the man he had just hit.

Blake moved his hands back and forth rapidly, pointing to the plates around him and the mess on the floor.

"We were going to clean it up in a minute. There's no need to act like that."

Blake raised his eyebrow at the man and rolled his eyes.

"Honestly, we were just going to get to it. There's no need to act like that, now, is there?"

Blake pointed to each man in turn and then pointed to the mess, snapping his fingers. He turned to leave but halted in his tracks. Signalling to the group again, he got the answer that he wanted.

"Yeah, Duke's in. Just follow the noise and you're bound to find him," said one of the men.

Blake walked out the way he came and tilted his head upwards. Rotating his head, like a bloodhound tracking a scent, he zeroed in on the sound that echoed around the building. He began to walk in that direction, nodding his head confidently.

The warehouse was in disarray, as usual, and he shook his head at the lumps of precious metals and gemstones just lying around. The lack of security measures never ceased to amaze him. Yes, they owned the local law enforcement, but that didn't mean they had to flaunt what they did in everyone's faces.

Blake opened a set of doors and walked down a flight of stairs. Reaching another door at the bottom, he pulled it open and walked down a corridor. The light flickered overhead and water dripped faintly, somewhere off in the distance. They were so wealthy they could allow water to go to waste like that. It made him sick. He came to another door and yanked it open.

A short shirtless male had his back to Blake. The person's back had what appeared to be a giant worm tattooed on it. The worm's mouth was open, attempting to swallow a red planet just above its head. Sweat glistened on his skin. Even from this angle, Blake could see that the person was breathing heavily.

"What is it, Blake?" Duke asked.

Blake walked around to face his boss. He took in the scene and gave a small shudder. Blood splattered the floor. Tied to a chair was an informant that Duke had caught before he could testify against the gang in a month or two's time. His gag was wet with tears and blood, and the smell of fear and urine hung heavily in the room.

Blake ran his scarred hands over the patchwork of scars on his face. Moving his hands rapidly back and forth in front of him, Blake informed Duke of what he had heard.

"Do you think this guy that attacked T back at Dusty's is someone from another gang? A gang from another city making a move against us?" said Duke.

Blake gave a noncommittal shrug and held his hands out in front of him.

"If one of those sons of whores wants a war, then a war we shall give them. I have come too far to be stopped. I shall destroy anyone that gets in my path." Duke cocked his arm back and slammed his fist into the informant's face. The blood on both his hands had already begun to dry, but that didn't seem to concern him.

"Did T say what this guy looked like?"

Blake pointed to his ear and allowed his hands to flow.

"Huge earring, huh? Well, put some credits out there and see what we can find out."

Blake took a step towards the door then stopped. He looked towards the informant and back at Duke. He raised one eyebrow in Duke's direction.

"What?"

Blake pointed towards the pipes lining the walls of the room like those of a church organ. Each one was hollow and open at the bottom, leading through the ceiling and beyond.

"The reason I made this room, Blake, is so that sound can travel around the whole base. Everything that happens here can be heard. Everyone that acts, thinks, or even has a subconscious thought against me–against the family–will know what will happen to them. Let the thuds and screams be a lesson to all!

"Now, find out who this fucker with an earring is. I think he needs to see the lovely features in this room."

11

The night was coming to an end–or just starting, depending on what side of the coin you viewed it from.

Phoenix and Saoirse were the only two left at the table. The others had left by the one or two, saying their good-nights. Neither said anything but simply drank and allowed the night to carry their thoughts into the breeze.

Phoenix wondered how he had managed to get mixed up in all of this. *One minute you're stealing money from a scumbag who sells drugs to school kids, and the next, you're on a distant planet stealing a ship from some gangster.*

No. Not stealing. Taking.

Phoenix had seen the passion and fire in L's eyes when she spoke about that ship. It meant the world to her. She had slaved over it. Put all her soul into it. To have it snatched away, while she was powerless to do anything about it, would, would...

Phoenix let out a sigh and allowed the thought to pass. No sense in working himself up about it now. He would need all his strength later. He looked over at Saoirse, whose eyes were slightly closed.

"Do you think L is going to be okay?" said Phoenix.

"Yes. I'll make sure of it," said Saoirse.

"She's trying to put a brave face on it, but I can understand the frustration of not being able to help a loved one. It hurts. It's hard to deal with. And no matter how many people offer words of comfort, it doesn't really help."

"Her race show their emotions through the colour of their hair. That's why it's so easy to tell what they're feeling."

"We have a saying back home: wearing your heart on your sleeve. It fits L perfectly."

Saoirse nodded slightly but still didn't move. Phoenix watched her for some time; it was akin to watching a lioness in the wild.

"You were quiet at the discussions. I would expect you to have the most valuable input among the whole crew," said Phoenix.

"Listening is more valuable than talking. Adding needless words just to partake in a conversation leads nowhere. Dooms us all. It's better to absorb the facts, allow them to sink in, then see what path lies ahead of you," said Saoirse.

Phoenix took a sip from his mug and felt a smile tug at the corners of his mouth.

"So where do you see the path leading us?" he asked.

"To blood and destruction."

The next day Phoenix and L walked side by side down a dusty track. They had left the others behind at Rusty's and said they would meet them back there later.

"What's this place we're going to called?" asked Phoenix.

"Game."

"Right. And we're going there...because? You didn't say much when you dragged me out of my room half naked."

"Game is a club where players go to play games."

Phoenix palmed himself in the face and shook his head. "Of course it is."

"Gaming is popular across many different galaxies and races. It's virtual reality taken to the next level. Whatever you want to play–or be–there is a game for it. It's grown so large that the stars of certain games are celebrities. Large amounts of credits are wagered when certain games or gamers are playing. In a lot of cases, gaming is the only way people can escape their poverty-stricken lives. But--"

"It comes at a cost?" said Phoenix.

"Yeah, it does. When certain bets go bad, or gamers themselves bet on themselves and lose, things can turn nasty."

"There's always someone looking to get a piece of the action."

"Yes, there is."

"You still haven't told me why we're going there, though," said Phoenix.

The pair sidestepped a couple of beggars with outstretched hands. L stopped in her tracks and looked left to right, a finger placed against her lips. She snapped her fingers and pointed down another street, walking in that direction.

"My brother, as you well know, loved computer programmes. He built some of the best known VRGs around--"

"VRG?" asked Phoenix.

"Virtual reality game. He had a knack for knowing just what players wanted in their games. What players needed to take their minds off life itself. But big brother sucked ass at the games he created. Any game, for that matter. Don't ask me how or why, but he just wasn't any good at them. Whatever game he touched he would lose at. People started to notice and place large bets against him that he couldn't pay."

"Don't tell me, that's where Duke comes in."

"Yup. When my brother couldn't pay off his debts, Duke demanded that he work for him, creating games that allowed the creator to say who won or who lost--"

"Ahh, smart. By rigging the games themselves, no one can blame or accuse Duke's men of cheating. I also take it he would lose a few big games, here and there, to make it seem legit?"

L nodded her head as they came to a large warehouse with flashing neon signs all over it.

"Subtle. Real fucking subtle," Phoenix said with a shake of his head.

Phoenix went through the sliding doors first, with L following close behind. The scene that met them jarred Phoenix's senses: a cacophony of flashing lights, sirens and excited whoops. The music from the overheard speakers mixed in with the sounds of the heaving crowd.

Rows and rows of what appeared to be beds stretched out on either side of them. People lay on them with helmets covering their faces. Holographic displays floated above each bed. A few flashed red, but most stayed a steady green. Occasionally lines of words scrolled down a few.

"The headsets are the VRGs. All these people playing are solo players, which means whatever they do in-game is private. There are a bunch of different games, each connected across many planets. It almost becomes a world in itself," said L.

"What do those flashing red lights mean?"

"A gamer has stayed in the game too long. He hasn't eaten or taken in any fluids. A message will warn the player in-game but most ignore it. It becomes addictive, being someone else."

"What happens when the player doesn't leave?" Phoenix asked.

"They get a second warning, and if they don't come out, then the game shuts down on them, kicking them out. They then can't go back in till the next day. It never used to be that way, but dying customers are not returning customers. This way," said L.

They moved through the crowd like farmers through a cornfield. Merchants offered to sell them anything from game cheat codes to food and drink. A few even offered stimulants to keep them awake.

Ahead of them, a huge crowd stared at hologram screens floating above their heads. It showed what appeared to be a gun battle going on between two gamers. People booed and cheered as the action took place. Phoenix saw bets being made and arguments breaking out over what was said.

The air was tense and heated.

Among the crowd, dotted about so they wouldn't draw too much attention, were security. Their worm tattoos told Phoenix who they worked for.

As one player got a clean head shot on his opponent, the crowd erupted in a roar.

Must be the crowd favourite.

The loser was pulled down from his game station by two unhappy-looking security guards and was pushed and shoved towards the back. By the amount of happy faces that clapped and cheered for the winner, the house must have lost big. Whatever debrief the loser was about to receive, Phoenix knew it would involve more fists than words.

"I think I see who we came to talk to," said L.

She pointed to a tall male with a ponytail, wearing all black. As they moved towards their man, he spotted them and took off running.

"I guess he doesn't want to talk," said Phoenix.

12

The man's ponytail flashed more colours than Phoenix could keep track of as they chased after him. He didn't have any trouble in pushing past people or using them as objects to shove in his pursuers' way.

Bodies flew over tables and slammed into screens.

Phoenix ran after him as the shouts and screams of pain were quickly left behind. He didn't let his attention waver as he jumped over a fallen body.

Ponytail kept up a pace that surprised Phoenix; he would expect the gamer to be out of shape from lying on his back all day. But Ponytail dodged and weaved and ducked, increasing the gap between him and Phoenix.

A waitress in a tight-fitting dress that left nothing to the imagination stepped back, and Phoenix grabbed her by one arm. "Sorry, beautiful, but do you think I can borrow that tray you're holding?"

The waitress smiled at Phoenix but he didn't wait for an answer. Taking the tray from her, he continued after his target. There were too many people in the way. He needed a clearer shot.

Phoenix kept his sights on Ponytail's fleeing back and leapt onto a stage. He heard shouts aimed at him, but he paid them no attention. Cocking his arm back, he threw the tray like a Frisbee, hoping for the best.

It didn't hit its intended target. Instead it struck someone else, who fell into Ponytail's way and knocked him off his feet.

"Good enough, I suppose," Phoenix said, leaping off the stage.

Ponytail picked himself back up and staggered towards the doorway. He didn't get there fast enough, and Phoenix's boot hit him square in the back. The impact sent him flying through the doors. Phoenix followed up with a kick to his ribs for good measure.

"I think my friend wants to speak to you," said Phoenix.

"And who would that be?"

"Her." Phoenix nodded at L as she made her way through the doors.

"I don't have anything to say to that whor--"

Phoenix delivered another kick to Ponytail's ribs, aiming for the same spot.

"Hello, Baldric," said L.

Phoenix snorted as he tried to keep a straight face.

"What?" said Baldric.

"You look like a fucking Baldric if I ever did see one," said Phoenix.

"Baldric, I want you to answer a few simple questions, and then we will let you be on your way."

"And why would I do that?"

L lowered herself so she was face to face with Baldric. "Because if you don't, my good friend over there will bash your brains out. Now, I don't like violence, and I have never fired a weapon of any sort, but you have information we need, and I want it."

"But--"

"And I will do whatever I have to do to get it."

"Listen, I understand how you feel. But... But..."

"Everything before the but is *bullshit*," said Phoenix.

Baldric's eyes darted from Phoenix to L. Licking his lips, he rose from his feet and brushed his jacket clean. "L! You know me. Me and you go way back. If you needed information, why didn't you just ask? I have always said what a good soul you are. Even when people were bad-mouthing your good name. Even when--"

"Where's Kai?" L asked.

Baldric sucked air through his teeth and scratched his scalp. "Come on, L. In the name of Soul, you know I would tell you anything but--"

The kick that Phoenix delivered to Baldric's kneecap buckled him, dropping him to the floor. Baldric grabbed it with both hands, shouting in pain.

"Everything before the but is *bullshit*," said Phoenix, rolling the last word on his tongue.

"Where is Kai?" L asked again.

"Okay. Okay. I don't know much. People ain't seen him around for a while. You know what he was like, you couldn't get him away from these machines. He was addicted. But after that business with you getting sent away--"

"You mean me being framed. You mean me going to Dredar for crimes I never committed! Everyone knew the truth, and no one said anything, or did anything to come to my aid--"

"Look, I never--"

"Is that what you mean? Because if it is, I would class it

as more than just some business. You know how many weeks and days I wasted! Do you know what I went through?"

L grabbed Baldric by his jacket lapels and glared into his face. Her eyes never left his. Her hair, a fiery crimson red, spoke of pain under the surface.

"Look, it wasn't my fault. I had nothing to do with it. I--"

"You did nothing about it. You *allowed* it to happen. You watched in the crowd like a faceless corpse. How long have we known each other, Baldric? How many years? You were my first kiss."

"I...know. Okay, look, all I know is that Kai is still with Duke. I don't know where he is holding him, but rumour has it that Duke still has him creating games. The last time anyone saw him was near Duke's compound. Near the shipyard. That's all I know."

L still held onto Baldric's lapels. Her glare was still glued to his face.

"That's all I know. I swear it," Baldric said, breaking her grip.

As the doors in front of them opened, four men with worm tattoos stepped out.

"I didn't tell her anything. I swear," Baldric said, running their way.

Whatever else Baldric said didn't matter, as a plasma bolt fired by one of the guards slammed into his chest.

"We've been looking for you," said one of the men to Phoenix, his plasma gun still smoking.

13

Phoenix drew his pistol and sent a volley of shots in the goons' direction. He didn't want to know why they were looking for him. He didn't really care. He took one look at Baldric's smoking remains and knew that the chat wasn't going to be a pleasant one. He grabbed L by the hand and they made their escape.

Shots peppered the ground around their feet as they zigzagged left and right. Phoenix brought his gun up and fired blindly behind him, hoping for the best, expecting the worst.

"Left–up ahead!" L gasped.

The crowd around them screamed and panicked as plasma bolts hit innocent bystanders. It didn't take long for everyone to duck and hide. Fear was thick in the air. Market stalls were overturned as people tried to make their escape. The stalls' contents spilled to the ground and were trampled underfoot.

"Right!"

Phoenix took the corner sharply, and a shot sailed over

his head, smashing a shop window. Its owner had the sense not to come out and investigate what was going on. Phoenix looked behind him and fired off a few more shots. As one hit its desired target he allowed himself a small smile.

At least that's one less to worry about.

"Why are they after us?" said Phoenix.

"Well...it may have something to do with you...blowing...one of their members' legs off," L gasped between breaths.

"Aw, man. They still mad about that? I thought they would have gotten over it, by now."

Another shop window exploded next to the pair, showering them with glass. Phoenix covered L as best as he could before returning fire.

"Do you have a plan?" asked L.

"When do I ever?"

They leapt over an overturned market stall as plasma bolts exploded around them.

"Was that guy really your first kiss?" Phoenix asked.

"Is this really the time?"

"No, but... Come on, L, you could have done so much better than a loser like--"

A plasma bolt took out a chunk of mortar next to Phoenix's head, forcing him to duck. He spun around and fired off what he could before his momentum brought him back around.

"Phoenix, I was young, and he was older. He appeared to be so... What do you what me to say? Like you have no partners in your past that you regret!"

"I can't say I do."

"Really?"

"No. All of my previous *lovers* were handpicked, like a

delicate flower, by me. They experienced something that will stay with them forever. Making love with me is really a curse if you--"

Phoenix felt another plasma bolt skim the top of his head, giving off the smell of singed hair.

"Argh! Enough of this," said Phoenix.

He looked ahead and saw a crane loaded with barrels. He waited until they had run past it to turn around and aim for the links that held it together. Firing at it repeatedly warped the metal, bringing down its contents and blocking their pursuers' path.

"That should hold them, for now. Let's make a move," said Phoenix.

"It won't be long till they are looking for us."

"We'll cross that bridge when we get to it... Was there really no one else?" said Phoenix.

"Shut up!"

Blake rubbed his scarred hands over his bald head as he walked. He stopped every so often and let out a heavy sigh. Rolling his tense neck, he heard it crack and pop. Finally he stood before an unmarked door, and once again he passed his hands over his head.

He lifted his hand to knock, but it paused midair. He brought it back down and scratched the back of his head. He straightened his clothes. He bit his lip. And still he didn't knock or enter.

His closed fist came up and stopped an inch away from the door. It hovered, it waited; for what, he didn't really know.

He let out a last sigh and his fist descended towards the door. The sound it made as it connected caused his heart to sink deeper than it already had.

"Enter!"

Blake did as he was told and walked into Duke's office.

Chaos wasn't the right word to describe the room.

Weapons of all shapes and sizes, from knives to guns and everything between, littered the office walls. A few were still blood-smeared. No, chaos wasn't the word that came to mind. Destruction was.

"Well?" asked Duke.

A frown crept over Blake's face. He waved his hands in front of him, disinterested in the information that he was giving.

"How much did we lose?"

Blake told him with a wave of his hand, as if it didn't matter.

"That's all of the day's takings. How could we lose so much at the VRG store? We had our best guy playing against some chump! All he had to do was play through the script! Just follow it. Did our boys take him outside and show him what we think of losers?" asked Duke.

Blake gave a small nod.

"Good. I don't want any of our boys to lose this week. We can't afford it. We need to make a profit. Make sure that Kai fixes whatever glitch made us lose that game."

Blake raised his eyebrow and threw out different hand gestures in quick succession.

"Whoa, whoa, you're going too fast. Who lost who?"

Blake slowed his hands down before ending his gesticulating monologue with fingers shaped like a gun firing into the air.

"It could only be one person that would ever want to

speak to Baldric. But she's... If this person with an earring was with her, then this could mean trouble. Not much, but you never know. Do you think she could be back?"

Blake gave Duke a small shrug.

"Whoever this earring fucker is, he seems to be quite capable. Injuring one of our guys and giving four others the slip is something not many people could do."

Blake rolled his eyes and shook his head.

"I know you may not think much of them, but they are the best men I can afford. Now, will you make sure that Kai fixes whatever glitch happened?"

Blake threw his hands up in the air and started to walk out the room.

"Blake, what's the matter? You've been acting strange lately," said Duke.

Blake turned on the spot and began to signal with force. His movements had no fluidity or flow. Each signal ended in a definite stroke. Each signal came down like a guillotine.

"What do you mean, I don't care about you?"

Blake pointed to himself again and shrugged his shoulders forward.

"Look, the business has taken up more of my time than I wanted it to, but that doesn't mean I care about you any less. It's just--"

Blake stamped his foot and turned away, marching towards the closed door.

Duke chased after him before he could open the door. Duke turned Blake around and lifted his head till they made eye contact.

"Look, things have been crazy around here lately, but why don't me and you go off world for a little bit, after this is all over? What you say?"

Blake brushed Duke's hand off his face and pointed to both of them before pulling his hands apart.

"I can't help that we've been growing apart. I'm trying to make amends, here. After the business--"

Blake turned on his heel and slammed the door behind him.

14

The crew sat around a table in a dark corner of Rusty's. L retold what had happened, as best she could, with Phoenix filling in the parts she missed. Half-finished drinks rested on the tables in front of them.

Phoenix passed his hand over his chin, sandpaper stubble greeting his palm. He took another sip of his drink and closed his eyes, breathing deeply. When was the last time he slept? It seemed like days had flown past, in the blink of an eye, since they had crash-landed on this planet.

The joy he had first felt at arriving here had all but disappeared. When people were shooting at you, you couldn't exactly enjoy the scenery.

"Where's Freyan?" said Phoenix.

"He said he needed supplies," replied Saoirse.

"What for?"

"How am I supposed to know?"

"I was just asking," said Phoenix.

Saoirse folded her arms over her chest and stared off into the distance.

What's her problem?

"I need to get my brother out of here," L said. "He's not safe, and I don't know how much longer he will be useful to Duke. Once Duke finds a replacement for him, it will all be over. Duke will kill him without a second thought. I need... I need---" She slammed her fist down on the table, toppling her drink over.

"Sorry," she said, wiping up the spilled contents.

"See, that's why I never had much to do with family," said Plowstow.

Out of the corner of his eye, Phoenix saw Saoirse's jaw set. Her hand began to tap along the handle of her knife.

"I mean, they're more hassle than they're worth. Me–if it was me–I would just leave him be. He got himself in this mess, he can get himself out. Siblings! Who needs them? You need to be more like me, L. I'm a survivor, a warrior--"

Saoirse shot up from where she sat, fire in her eyes. Phoenix had seen it coming, and held down the hand that was beginning to draw her knife. She looked at him with a snarl on her lips. Phoenix kept his hand firm and simply shook his head.

"Dishonourable--" Saoirse began, but cut herself off. She slapped Phoenix's hand away and stormed out, shoving aside anyone unlucky enough to get in her way.

"What's her problem?" Plowstow asked.

"Let me take a guess, you dick! Your utter lack of compassion for anyone apart from yourself. Your selfishness. Your downright lack of sensitivity to anyone's feelings. Your total lack of respect for your crewmates--"

"I didn't ask--"

"I know you didn't ask, Plowstow! But like it or lump it, we're all you've got. Now, you either shape up or ship out. It's your choice! No one is forcing you to be here. You're free to leave, whenever you like," said Phoenix.

Plowstow shot from his chair, forcing it back, and it landed on the floor with a bang. "Well, if that... I can't... Have it your way."

Plowstow turned on his heel and walked away from them, chest puffed up, arms swinging like pendulums in grandfather clocks.

"Well, that could have gone better," said Phoenix.

L said nothing but simply stared into her now empty glass. The other customers went back to their conversations and drinks, and the noise slowly started to rise. The show was over; there was nothing interesting to gawk at.

"What's up with Saoirse?"

"She's upset that she wasn't there when we went to the VRG store. She can be a bit prideful, sometimes."

"This captain shit is a pain in the ass. They always make it look so easy in the movies. Argh. It's like dealing with a bunch of children."

Phoenix rubbed his face and stared at the ceiling, hoping to find the answers to his problems there.

L whispered, "When I was younger, I always thought that the older you got, the more you knew, and the easier everything would become. But the older I get, the more I realise how little I know."

"L, I am many things. A lot of those things are not nice. But I am a man of my word, and when I told you I would protect you, and make sure that nothing bad would ever come of you, I meant it. We will find your brother and get him back. Okay?"

"Okay."

15

Holger lay sprawled on what appeared to be a sofa with wheels, while two of his slaves–or servants, as he called them–pulled him along. A small fan blew a cooling mist on his face. He tilted his head back and let out a small sigh. He could use any one of the automated vehicles to drive him anywhere he wanted to go on the ship, but being pulled along had a certain personal touch.

Who was he, to walk like some commoner? Like some low-born bastard birthed on some smugglers' ship. No, he would use all the available power at his disposal. More fool those that didn't.

"Take me to the conference room. I have an urgent meeting with my father. No doubt he wants to congratulate me on all my recent successes."

The servants looked at each other, smirks threatening to burst from the corners of their mouths.

Servants and guards alike lowered their heads as Holger was pulled along. Not a head that they passed was bowed fully. Some barely managed a slight nod. Most had barely-hidden smirks; all had looks of disgust.

"Hurry! I must not be late for my appointment with Father. He needs my counsel."

One of the servants pulling Holger along turned his laughter into a coughing fit. He slapped his chest and looked up at Holger. "Sorry, my lord. I don't feel all too well lately."

"Hmm–see to it or I will replace you. Can't stand the sick."

Stopping at the door to the conference room, Holger got up and allowed his eyes to travel down his body. "How do I look?" he asked the two servants.

Scuffed and watermarked shoes were barely covered by wrinkled trousers. His uniform blazer sat lumpily, the buttons stretched to breaking point, as the cloth struggled to contain his bulging stomach. Food stains marked his cuffs.

"You cut a fine figure, sir."

"Dashing, if I may say so," replied the other.

"I thought as much," said Holger.

He walked into the conference room and was greeted by a hologram of a man standing with his hands behind his back. His salt and pepper hair was cut short and a slight scar ran the length of his jaw. Seeing Holger approach, he clenched his jaw, making the scar ripple. His uniform was finely pressed and hugged the contours of his body like a second skin. Gleaming medals sat at his breast pocket, and the pocket displayed the image of a hand gripping chain links and the family motto: We never forget.

"Ajax, where is Father?"

Ajax breathed heavily through his nose before responding. "He is unavailable at the present time."

"Unavailable? Unavailable!"

"Yes, Holger, unavailable. It means he can't be here at the present time. It means--"

"I know what it means, you dolt."

Ajax raised an eyebrow slightly but said nothing.

Holger paced up and down, stomping his feet like a child. "He knows what today is. What's so important that he had to miss talking to me?"

"He is...sparring. Training--"

"Sparring! Fucking sparring! Is this a joke, Ajax? No, how can it be? He always preferred that to me. He always preferred many things to me. I would like to speak with him. Can you get him for me?"

"Holger, it isn't the best time, right now. After losing Earth's resources...your father has to review things and try and regain what he lost. That task in itself is proving more difficult than he would have thought.

"Plus, with the Council digging into everyone's affairs, things are strained, right now. There are big plays being made by unknown players in the shadows. Your father needs a clear head and some time to decide what to do next."

"But, Ajax...it's my birthday. I thought..."

"Things like birthdays will have to wait for another time, I am afraid, young master."

"But Earth wasn't my fault. How was I supposed to know it would end up the way it did? Smit failed me. It was out of my hands. Surely Father sees that?"

"He--"

"You must *make* him see that I tried my hardest. It wasn't my fault. I tried, but things just didn't work out like they should have done."

Ajax's face turned to stone and all pity left his eyes.

"I am making amends," Holder said. "I have my best people working on it. That bastard who ruined our plans will learn what it means to cross a Portendorfer. He will--"

The hologram of Ajax disappeared, and the last image Holger was left with was of Ajax shaking his head in disgust.

16

Plowstow walked with his head bowed and hood up. Glancing furtively behind him, he stopped in doorways, every so often, and counted to ten. Satisfied that no one was following him, he continued on. Resting his hand on the pistol on his hip gave Plowstow some security. It wasn't much, but it would do.

The dark shadows lurking in the mouths of alleyways took a step back as Plowstow exposed the gun at his side. Sidestepping over the occasional dead animal, Plowstow fixed his gaze forward and marched on.

He came to a stop under the fading red sign of a boarded-up shop. Pulling his cloak around him, Plowstow slipped into a groove in the wall and waited. His breath billowed out before him, and he pulled his cloak tighter around him.

Fuck this planet! The days were humid, and hotter than working on a mining ship on Rar, but the nights were cold enough to freeze the blood in your veins.

Click, click, click.

Plowstow tightened his grip on the handle of his pistol

and drew back further into the shadows. He held his breath and waited. He didn't move from his spot for fear of being found. Tilting his head into the breeze that swept past him, carrying any sound, he listened and waited.

But still nothing came.

Night must be playing tricks.

A sound to his left made him draw his pistol. Rapid breaths were expelled from his body, running away from him like wild horses. Plowstow scanned the darkness in front of him, searching, looking.

He could have sworn that he had heard something.

Maybe...

"You're getting jumpy in your old age," whispered a voice just behind his ear.

Plowstow whipped round bringing his pistol to bear, but was stopped short as the barrel of a gun was placed under his chin. It hummed slightly with power.

"Now, now, big boy. We wouldn't want to do anything rash, would we?"

Plowstow tried to swallow but his mouth had become dry. He licked his lips and stared at the person in front of him. Orange hair fell just below her ears in a short bob. Smooth green skin was pulled tight over a lean, muscled frame. Slight curves stood out against the leather outfit she wore. Her canines shone in the darkness. Inviting, welcoming, hungry.

"Odessa," said Plowstow.

"Plowstow, darling, how have things been?"

"Good. But it would go a lot better if you took that damn pistol out of my face."

Odessa tilted her head slightly and gave Plowstow a smirk. The pistol still remained.

"I thought we were here to do business," Plowstow said.

"I ain't got all day, you know. Got things to do. People to see. Credits to make. I can take my business elsewhere, if you ain't interested."

"Plowstow, Plowstow, Plowstow." Odessa accompanied every word with a pat on the side of Plowstow's face.

"What?"

"How did you ever survive out there?" she asked.

"What?"

"I don't mean on this rotten planet. I mean among the stars. Someone like you should have died years ago. If there ever was a god, you should be paying them for their kindness in regards to your health."

"I do just fine, thank you. I have survived for this long because of my smarts."

Odessa brought a hand to her mouth to hold back a snort. Shaking her head, she looked left and right. Not seeing any threats, she lowered her gun slightly but didn't put it away.

"What took you so long? I been waiting here in this stinking alley for what feels like forever. This is bad--"

"Don't lie, honey. I saw your scared little form jumping at every little shadow. You haven't been here long," said Odessa.

"How do you know that?"

"Because I know everything, darling." Odessa smiled.

Plowstow scratched his groin before giving Odessa a look of disdain. "You have my credits?"

"Maybe. You have the product?"

"What do you take me for, some fool? You'll get to see the product when I see the right amount of credits."

Odessa let out a sigh and brought the holocom on her wrist to her face. She punched in some numbers and a projection formed in the air between the two of them. It displayed numbers that brought a smile to Plowstow's face.

"Very nice," said Plowstow.

"Now. Can I see what I am buying?"

Plowstow let out a bark of laughter before shaking his head. "You think I'm that stupid? To bring it here?"

"Well, the thought did cross my mind."

"I will message you a time and a place to do the deal. A crowded place. I have heard how you treat people you do business with. Until then, stay on the planet, and I will be in touch soon."

Plowstow made his way back the way he had come with a smile on his face. Things were finally going his way.

17

Phoenix made his way up a flight of stairs toward the rooms they were staying in. They had managed to secure rooms above Rusty's, after Saoirse had a quiet chat with the landlord. Whatever had been said was lost on Phoenix, but there had been much head nodding and smiling from the owner.

Footsteps echoing on the wooden floor brought Phoenix out of his reverie.

Saoirse descended towards him, her face expressionless. Phoenix stopped and watched her stride towards him. She was beautiful. Her hair flowed like a lion's mane, and her walk was confident, powerful, sure.

Phoenix watched her outfit hug her figure, showing the outlines of her curves. He traced each peak and valley, lost for a moment in the amusement park that was her body.

"You're blocking the way."

"What?" said Phoenix with a jerk.

"You're blocking the way. I suggest you move," said Saoirse.

Phoenix swallowed hard and took a deep lungful of stale

air to try and clear his head. "There was something I wanted to talk to you about..." Phoenix said, his gaze once again trailing where it shouldn't.

"Which was?"

"Err...yes. Yes. I just wanted to apologise for not inviting you along, to come with me and L to the VRG store. We could have used your help."

"Yes, you could have."

"We could have used your help, but I honestly didn't think it was going to turn out how it did. I should have run it past the crew to see what they thought about the idea. Or at the very least I should have told you where we were going. I don't think we will ever be able to trust one another if we don't start sharing. Talking as a group. Making decisions as a group," said Phoenix.

Saoirse nodded her head slowly, a slight hint of a smile tugging at the corners of her lips. "I completely agree. With that said, I must inform you that I have found information on Kai's whereabouts and was planning to head there tomorrow night."

"By yourself..."

"Yes. I thought that would have been best."

"You always need someone to watch your back. I'll tag along. And I know you may not want to, but I think we should take L." Phoenix held up his hand when he saw the look Saoirse gave him. "I don't think she will ever forgive either of us if she doesn't get to tag along. Do you want to tell her that she will be staying behind?"

"No, I wouldn't. There would be a lot of crying and tantrums involved," Saoirse said with a sigh.

"Don't worry, she will be fine," said Phoenix.

I hope, he thought, as he made his way past Saoirse.

Phoenix spotted Freyan sitting at a table by himself. A cloak covered most of his features. The only thing that gave him away was his white hands. Phoenix pulled up a chair and sat down in front of him.

"Penny for your thoughts?"

"Penny...for your...thoughts?" said Freyan.

"Its an Earth saying. It means what's on your mind. What are you thinking about?" Phoenix asked.

"Oh, Earth sayings. Yes. Well, what I am thinking about would probably bore you. Or you wouldn't possibly understand."

"With you being a highly evolved and intelligent race, you mean. Your thoughts alone would confuse and frighten a small mind such as mine?"

"Exactly."

They both looked at each other before breaking out in quiet laughter.

Phoenix spotted a barmaid with light blue skin and waved her over. She had a twinkle in her eye, and she gave him a dazzling smile. She gently touched Phoenix's shoulder as she positioned herself close to him. She was that close Phoenix could feel the heat she gave off, and a sweet honeysuckle smell drifted off her like the mist off a cold December shore.

"What will you have to drink?" she asked.

"I will have whatever you think is best that won't kill me. This is my first time on this beautiful planet, so show me what the drink of choice is," said Phoenix.

"Hah! I would hardly call this rock beautiful."

"It all depends on who's doing the looking, I guess."

The barmaid bit her bottom lip and gave Phoenix a

thoughtful look before saying, "I'll bring something over that I think you'll like. It's sweet to the taste and light to the touch."

"That sounds just what I am looking for."

With that, the barmaid let them be.

"It amazes me that even this far from Earth most of the species I have encountered look so alike. I mean, L could pass for a human. Not only her but many that I have seen along the way. Different skin tones, yes, but not that much different," said Phoenix.

"The universe is endless, Phoenix. Are you really that surprised that you may meet some races that look like you? Or some races that couldn't be further apart? There seems to be a general rule of thumb that most races you encounter will be bipedal. That's the most common trait, it seems, when it comes to how races evolve. But that isn't always the case. The Rocha are made up of mostly rock. And don't get me started on the insect races. The point is, there are many wonders that you have yet to see–that even I have yet to see. Let's just hope we live long enough to see them."

"So with regards to interspecies relations..." said Phoenix.

Freyan gave Phoenix a blank stare from under his cloak as the silence between them stretched out.

"You know, making the beast with two backs. Doing the old bedroom shaker. Waking the neighbours with the headboard banger."

"I don't follow you."

Phoenix raised both hands in the air and made one hand a circle and slid his finger in and out of it.

"Oh! You mean coitus."

"Well, it doesn't sound sexy when you say it like that, but yes. Regarding that...will there be complications if I chose to spend the evening with a female who isn't human?"

"If they look like you, walk like you, and smile at you, then it should be okay. You should stay away from certain races, because the females eat their sexual partners after mating. But you will know what one of those looks like when you see it," said Freyan, rising from his seat.

"Oh, that reminds me. I haven't seen you around here much. Not getting into any trouble, I hope," said Phoenix.

"Me? No, dear friend, I would do nothing of the sort. I have just been getting...supplies that we will need when we get off this rock," Freyan said, walking away.

Phoenix leaned back in his chair and pondered Freyan's response. Something didn't feel right about it, but just now he had enough on his plate to worry about. Freyan's comings and goings would have to wait for another day.

A gentle touch on his shoulder brought him out of his thoughts.

"I can't seem to find the drink of choice behind the bar, but I remembered I may still have some up in my room..." The barmaid smiled.

"Won't you be missed?"

"Tia is covering me."

"Then lead the way. I am dying to try something with some homegrown flavour."

"I was hoping you would say that," said the barmaid, taking Phoenix by the hand.

18

He was here again.

The same place he told himself that he wouldn't be. The same place he told himself he would never see. The same place his feet always brought him. No matter how hard his brain tried to tell him that he shouldn't be there. No matter how hard his gut rumbled and protested at the image he saw.

Blake ran his scarred hands over his face. He breathed in and out slowly. His heart raced. He wiped his sweaty hands on the front of his top. He licked his cracked lips but his mouth was dry.

Today was the day. It would all change after he had his conversation with Duke. It would be better. He would gain his freedom again. Duke would see reason.

Today was the day.

It would be the last time he saw that damn door!

Today was the day.

Blake lifted his hand and tapped lightly–once–and with it his heart picked up an extra pace.

"Enter!"

Blake grabbed the handle of the door and placed his other hand over the top of the first to stop it from shaking. Taking another deep breath, he pushed the door open.

"Ahh, there you are. Good. I have a few things to discuss with you," Duke said, sitting behind his desk.

Blake held out his hand and began to sign but was cut short by Duke.

"Blake, I'll hear what you have to say in a minute, but this is important. I think gangs from different cities have been attacking some of our men out near the digging sites. I think we may need to place more men out there."

Blake's jaw grew taut, and he fixed Duke with a glare.

"What?"

Blake gave Duke a few hand signs before throwing his hands up in the air.

"I know we don't have the men, but those water territories are important. If we lose those, we may as well say goodbye to our hold on this city. Those territories are our lifeline to survival. They're the most important thing that we have."

Blake shook his head, hands waving in front of him as he paced toward Duke's desk. Standing in front of it, he placed both hands on the desk.

"Look, I know we lost men. I know we've had to go deeper and deeper into worm country, but that's where all the untapped underground lakes are."

Blake slammed his fist on the table and turned his back, making his way towards the office door.

"Blake! What is this about?"

Blake stopped in his tracks, head low, but didn't turn around.

"Look, we have to get the water somehow. What do you want me to do?"

Blake spun around and pointed out the window, to one of the large floating orbs in the sky.

"Why not dig this close to the city?" said Duke. "If the resources are here, it would be stupid not to. What are a few worm attacks? Once you're behind the city walls, you're protected anyway. Plus, no one should be leaving the city. We have everything anyone could need right here. The warnings have gone out. People know the risk. It's on them if they chose to ignore them."

Blake's shoulders rose and fell as he stared at a person he no longer knew.

"My promise still stands. After all this is over, it will just be me and you. One long holiday. Maybe to one of the resort planets," said Duke.

Blake continued to stare, hands down at his sides.

"Blake, I mean it."

Blake shook his head once, twice, and then he was gone, walking through the door that now made his skin crawl.

Today was meant to be the day.

But as Blake's footsteps carried him further and further away from Duke's office, he knew that it wasn't going to be.

19

Phoenix peered at the scene ahead of him with a slight frown on his face. Zipping his jacket up, he allowed it to hug his body, protecting him against the night air that threatened to steal the breath from his lungs. He flexed his numb fingers so the blood flowed through them and warmed them. He looked towards Saoirse. "I thought you said that security would be light on the ground."

"This *is* light," said L. "Normally, there would be a whole squad of men just milling about. But Duke must truly own the city if he only needs one man to stand guard."

"L is correct. From my observations of the building, this is our best time," said Saoirse.

Phoenix scratched his growing stubble. The building seemed to be an abandoned warehouse. Some glass windows were shattered; others were left open. The whole building just didn't seem to be in use.

The only thing that gave it away was the occupied guard station in front of it. Behind, the warehouse loomed like a mountain of metal in the distance. Scrap heaps were piled high as far as the eye could see. Among the metal heaps, the odd ship shone like a jewel sticking out of the dirt. Most of them looked to be out of commission–rust buckets that had barely stood the test of time.

A few, though, stood out like sore thumbs: sleek in body, with powerful thrusters sticking out the back, and weapon turrets adorning every inch of available space.

"Would you look at those," said Phoenix, letting out a low whistle.

"Crime pays," said L.

"So I've heard."

"We should be going. The routines of the guards are never predictable," said Saoirse.

"Alright. Let's do this," said Phoenix.

They moved as one towards the guard station. Phoenix and Saoirse drew their weapons, sweeping the area ahead of them. They stopped periodically to scan the surrounding area. Although it appeared to be quiet, appearances tended to be deceiving.

They stopped at the mouth of an alley. They could go no further without being seen. They would have to cross an open area, which would allow the guard to see them and alert anyone else of their presence before they got to him.

"Thoughts?" Phoenix asked Saoirse.

"On it."

Saoirse took out what appeared to be two clear balls attached by a length of rope. Pressing the centre of each ball made them pulse red. Twirling the balls above her, she locked her gaze on the target ahead of her. Released at full swing the balls sped through the air with a slight hum.

The guard looked towards the direction of the weapon

but it was too late. They hit him square in the chest, wrapping round his torso. He began to utter a yell but it was cut short as electricity leapt from the balls and danced along his body. As he fell face first in the dirt, the only sound that could be heard was the thud of his body smacking the ground.

Saoirse looked through the scope of her weapon, she held her fist clenched, signalling her companions to remain stationary. She waved the others forward and they began to move towards the building.

"Are we just going to walk right through the front door?" L asked.

"No. There's a entrance to the side that would serve us better," said Saoirse.

They stopped at the body of the fallen guard and saw that he was still out for the count. Phoenix went to grab him by the foot and stopped.

"Is this still live?" he asked.

"No, the current should have passed by now," said Saoirse.

"Should have?"

"Stop being an infant. Your incessant worrying will not change matters."

"Incessant. Infant."

Phoenix shook his head and grabbed a hold of one of the guard's boots. His body convulsed uncontrollably and he let out a soft groan. Panic crossed Saoirse's face, and she rushed to his aid, stopping halfway when she saw the smile plastered across Phoenix's face.

"Worried?" Phoenix asked.

Saoirse's nostrils flared as she took a step towards him, free hand clenched in a fist, and she was only stopped by L stepping in between the pair.

"If you two don't mind, I would like to get my brother back while he's still alive."

"Sorry," they both muttered.

Phoenix dragged the limp body out of sight and made sure that he was gagged and tied. They didn't want any unwelcome surprises while this mission was underway. As he walked away, he heard a slight moan behind him. Turning back around, he saw that the guard was beginning to stir. Phoenix delivered a punch that made the guard's head bounce on the ground like a basketball.

"Stay down."

The trio moved silently around the building. They stopped every so often to check their surroundings. Nothing stirred in the dead of night but animals that scuttled from one hole in the wall to the next. Moving to a rusty door, Saoirse began to unpack items from her person.

"What are you doing?" asked Phoenix.

"Opening the door," she said, slotting metal tools into one another like a jigsaw puzzle.

"Allow me," said Phoenix, grabbing the handle of the door and pulling it towards him.

Phoenix wanted to smirk. He could feel the corners of his mouth twitch but he didn't dare. It would be one smirk too many, the one that would push Saoirse over the edge.

"After you," said Phoenix.

Saoirse tried her best to swallow the look of anger that flashed across her face but couldn't manage it. Her nostrils still flared despite her best efforts.

"Thank... you," said Saoirse.

L ignored them both and took a step into the darkness without a backwards glance their way.

"L," Phoenix and Saoirse said as one.

But it was no use. She was already lost in the darkness.

Vanishing from them right before their eyes, she was swallowed up whole.

Phoenix and Saoirse each mirrored the other's worried expression before they made their way into the darkness after her.

20

Darkness engulfed Phoenix's senses; it was as if he was trapped under the ocean with no way out. He halted his steps and took deep calming breaths to slow his racing heart. Slowly, his eyesight adjusted to the gloom around him.

Saoirse stood a few feet away from him, hand on her pistol, scanning the room. She appeared to have adjusted to the darkness a lot quicker than he had.

Phoenix looked for any sign of L. There was none. Swearing under his breath, he saw two doors that she might have gone through. Pointing to himself, Phoenix gestured to one door. He pointed to Saoirse and gestured to the other. She nodded her head in understanding and took off.

Phoenix would have liked the group to stay together, but there was nothing for it now. With L nowhere to be found, their first task was to find her–then her brother. He just hoped that neither got themselves killed before they could be saved.

Phoenix walked towards his allocated doorway. He swept his plasma pistol in front of him. He wished he had something with a bit more punch. But being down on credits, and not being able to salvage much from their downed ship, had left them with few options when it came to weaponry.

Saoirse, on the other hand, seemed to be a walking armoury. That woman went to bed with more weapons on her then she did clothes. He didn't know where she kept them.

Phoenix came to the arch of the doorway and tried to get a better picture of what lay beyond. Nothing screamed danger. But in this darkness he didn't want to take any unnecessary chances.

He held his breath as he walked through the door. He looked left, then right, but the coast seemed clear. Phoenix spun around as he heard movement behind him but couldn't see anything. He wanted something to come at him as he scanned the darkness. He wanted something to break the tension that was so thick you could practically swim in it.

Just rats. Or the space equivalent.

Phoenix kept his pistol level and continued on. Plates of food were clustered here and there. Someone had half attempted to clean them up, but most had been left stacked in a corner.

His foot knocked something that clattered to the floor.

Shit.

Trying to stop it from making a noise was pointless. The sound had escaped and was bouncing from wall to wall like a five-year-old hopped up on sweets.

Phoenix stayed motionless, waiting for something–anything–but nothing came. He continued on regardless. He was in too deep, now. Too committed to turn back. Walking past a sofa, he spotted what appeared to be a bundle of clothes on it. Giving it a quick once-over he continued on.

He didn't hear the footsteps. He felt the hands grip him from behind. He was unable to do anything to prevent being thrown off his feet.

Phoenix landed heavily amongst a pile of food scraps, which covered him from head to toe. "Ugh."

He reached for his pistol but it was nowhere to be found. Looking up he saw a brute of a Tingoneese coming his way. He was covered from head to toe in tattoos. A worm eating what appeared to be a doll took up a portion of his face.

"Ain't you an ugly fucker," said Phoenix.

"You'll look worse than me after I'm done with you," the brute growled.

Phoenix was about to respond but thought it would be better to roll out of the way of the oncoming boot making its way towards his face. He leapt to his feet in a fluid roll and threw a punch that connected with a thump. Looking at the gang member in front of him he expected some sort of reaction. But what he got was laughter.

Worm Face held his stomach as rolls of laughter escaped him. Shaking his head he waved Phoenix on. He stood with his hands on his hips, a smile on his face, waiting for Phoenix's next move.

Not one to waste an opportunity, Phoenix took a running swing at the man's face. This time, he was rewarded with a grunt.

Worm Face staggered backwards and just about kept his legs underneath him.

"Why you no laugh?" Phoenix mocked.

Worm Face wiped blood dripping from his nose and came at Phoenix with a roar.

Phoenix ducked a left and then a right cross and threw a

kick to his opponent's kneecap. The satisfying sound of it popping out of place brought a grim smile to his face. He threw his own punches that landed, but nothing seemed to hurt the monster.

As Worm Face grabbed Phoenix in a bear hug, Phoenix felt the air whoosh from his lungs. He tried to struggle free but the more he moved, the worse it became. Every movement he made felt like agony. Black spots danced in front of his vision.

"Seems like I'll get the last laugh," said a voice that sounded like it was in the distance.

With a roar, Phoenix brought his mouth down on his attacker's shoulder and bit into it for all he was worth. The scream that escaped Worm Face's lips could have shattered glass.

Phoenix slipped from his grip and landed on all fours. He grabbed Worm Face by the legs and brought the brute down on his back. Phoenix mounted him and rained down blow after blow.

Worm Face bucked like a stallion, trying to dislodge Phoenix. As Worm Face turned belly down, Phoenix sunk in a choke, shutting off the blood supply to the man's brain. He was unconscious in what felt like a blink of an eye.

Phoenix got up and saw his pistol a hand's reach away from him. "Typical."

Sobs of anguish cut through his train of thought. He picked up his pistol and checked it still worked before making his way to the cries that beckoned him into the darkness.

21

Phoenix crept forward, drawn to the childlike sobs. The plan was to sneak into the building silently, unnoticed. But that plan had flown out the window when he had been attacked. The scuffle had created enough noise to raise the dead. No doubt everyone now knew something was up and was on high alert.

Phoenix continued picking his way onward with care. The cries seemed to be getting closer. He flicked his gaze from left to right; nothing jumped out at him but dusty walls.

Phoenix stopped in his tracks as he saw a small body ahead of him.

Is that...?

He moved closer until the outline of L formed before him. She had her hand on the handle of a door, but she seemed frozen in time. He walked towards her but still she didn't move. She didn't turn as his footsteps approached. She simply stared at the closed door ahead of her.

"L?"

She didn't turn at the sound of her name. The only thing that escaped her lips were tearful sobs.

"L, what's the matter?" Phoenix asked, finally reaching her side.

"I..." She turned her head his way and even in the gloom he could see her red-rimmed eyes. "I..." She shook her head and wiped her nose on her sleeve. "What if I find something I wish I hadn't? What if I get all this way and...and...and he's dead?" L spoke as if her thoughts on the matter were final. As if there was no other outcome that she could foresee.

"And what if he's not?" said Phoenix.

"I don't think I want to know the answer, Phoenix. I don't think I want to face whatever is behind this door. If I never find out, then everything can still be how it used to be. I can still have the memories of us playing as kids. I can still have the memories of us being happy. Before all this happened."

"Look, I would never force you to do something that you don't want to. But if you don't find out now, if you don't face this fear, then you'll regret it forever. Trust me. From a man who has more than a few regrets in his past: it will haunt you forever."

"I guess you're right." L took a deep breath before giving Phoenix a shaky smile. "Shall we?"

L turned the handle and pushed open the door. A smiling face greeted them on the other side.

"Big sis! Where you been?"

22

Holger sat in a leather chair with a glass of alcohol in one hand and a leather whip in the other. Taking a sip from his crystal cup he savoured the flavour in his mouth before swallowing it. It danced on his tongue and numbed his throat as it made its way down.

He tilted his head back and closed his eyes at the injustice of it all. He was simply trying to please his father, but no matter what he did, the old man wouldn't be satisfied. It was as if Holger was destined to forever be out of his favour.

No matter what he said he would do.

No matter what he did.

No matter how much he achieved.

Lord Portendorfer was not someone to give his approval easily. He had once. When it came to *those two,* he gave it as freely as breathing. But even then, Holger was never on the receiving end of those sugar-coated words.

Now Holger was stuck on this floating prison of a ship, making his way back to a planet that his father had sent him to–to look after it. *Look after! Hah!* More like he wanted Holger out of the way. If his father would only listen to him–

talk to him–Holger would show him that things were not as dire as he thought.

Yes, Holger had lost Earth's resources, but so what? There were more planets out there than the Council could keep track of, and if the family got to them first, the Council would be none the wiser. His father was getting soft in his old age. It was time for Holger to take over the family. He was the first son. He was the only son. He was the rightful heir. The longer his father went on belittling him, the more pain his father would face when Holger's time for power came.

Blood dripped from the tip of the whip onto the floor.

A buzzing from Holger's wrist brought him out of his dreamlike state and into the present. He punched a code into his holocom and an image of Rustem presented itself before him.

"I hope you have good news, Rustem. For your sake."

"Good news to me may not be good news to you...*my lord*," said Rustem.

Holger took another sip from his drink and allowed the silence to spread between them for a moment. Muffled cries in the distance threatened to spoil that.

"So what have you found out?"

"I have found out a great--"

"About what I assigned you to," snapped Holger.

"Oh, that. Well, you will be pleased to know that victory is almost at hand. Victory has such a funny meaning, doesn't it? It's a pretty way of saying conquer. Dominate. Get what you want--"

"Yes. Yes, I admit it does. But you still haven't told me why I should be pleased. That is the part I am most eager to hear," said Holger.

"Sometimes the joy of the moment is better than the

moment itself. You should learn that, if you ever wish to be in power, or, more importantly, *stay* in it. I have learnt that Phoenix and his crew have landed on Tingo and will be there for some time," Rustem said, playing with a bell attached to his hair.

"How far away from their location are you?" Holger asked, leaning in closer.

"I am on the planet as we speak. This should be over in a matter of days. A week, at the most."

Holger took another sip from his drink, swallowed, and smiled. "The quicker it is done, the better paid you will be."

"I understand. Would you like a souvenir to show that the job is completed? His ear, maybe?"

"I didn't want anything, but now that you have mentioned it, that sounds like a brilliant idea. How did you know?"

"You seemed like the type that would," said Rustem, cutting off the call before anything more could be said.

Holger finished off the remainder of his drink and got to his feet. The whip trailed along the floor, leaving a bloody stain wherever it touched. One of Holger's servants hung from the ceiling, gagged and bound. The result of his lashes could be seen all over her naked form. Open. Bleeding. Peeling.

Standing in front of her, he placed his hands on his hips. "Now, I am going to teach you what it means to not bring me the right food that I ordered. After I am done with you, it will be a lesson that you will never forget."

23

L's face contorted as a million different emotions crossed her features. Her fists, down at her sides, opened and closed repeatedly. Her chest rose and fell as she struggled to keep her emotions in check. Her cheek twitched and she closed her eyes to the sight in front of her.

Phoenix looked towards the men in front of them, then back at L. "L, you okay?"

L didn't say anything as she stood rooted to the spot.

"L, what's wrong?" asked her brother.

"What's wrong? What's wrong?! What's wrong! I'll tell you *what's wrong*, Kai. I haven't seen you in *how* long, and you act like I just went to the shops! Where's the joy at seeing your sister back, safe and sound? Where is the panic that you felt because I had been gone for so long? Where is the...I don't know! Emotion!" L made her way closer to Kai with each sentence she uttered. Her hair was the colour of a burning forest on a pitch-black night.

"Whoa, whoa. Where is all this coming from, sis? This

ain't like you. Relax. Enjoy this moment of bliss. Enjoy this moment for what it is--"

"Are you fucking with me?" L hissed, spittle flying from her mouth.

"In the name of Soul, there's no need to use language like that. I mean, it's been a while, but come on, L. The faith of Soul works in mysterious ways. I knew you would be back in no time."

L slapped Kai with all her might. The sound echoed around the room and Phoenix felt it. It didn't have the high ringing tone that one would expect from a slap. The sound was deep and the slap was meant to hurt; it was meant to be felt.

L rubbed her hand and took a step back from Kai.

Kai kept his hand to his cheek trying to soothe the pain. Eyes wide, mouth slightly open, he tried to speak but seemed at a loss for words. Kai walked towards L, shaking his head, and tried to smile, but that was the wrong thing to do.

Phoenix saw the tension in L's shoulders. He could see her hands still curled up, wanting to unleash hell. The hair colour should have given it away to Kai. The hard stare that didn't shift or lower should have been a warning. The small growl that escaped L's throat should have stopped him in his tracks.

But Kai kept coming.

Phoenix could have jumped in sooner. He knew what was going to happen, but he felt like Kai needed to take a few lumps before the conversation could really get underway. Kai's easy-going and carefree attitude had a time and a place, but now wasn't it.

The first few swings of L's fists landed across Kai's jaw, sending him sprawling backwards. He tried to shield himself as best as he could, but the blows came fast and hard. L hit everywhere she could–his head, body, arms. It didn't matter to her. The frustration and anger that had built up over time needed some release.

"You selfish, uncaring, VRG loser," L spat.

Phoenix walked over slowly and grabbed her by the waist. He lifted the pint-sized ship's engineer up from behind and pulled her away from her brother.

"Phoenix, let me go!"

L fought Phoenix with strength he didn't think she had. Her legs still kicked and her arms still swung at her target. Any other time, the image would have appeared hilarious to Phoenix, but not right then.

He could feel L's hot tears dripping onto his arm. He could feel the cries of pain finally bubbling up to the surface as small shudders swept through L's body.

"Do you know...what I have been through?" L whispered. Her movements stilled and she hung in Phoenix's arms like a puppet with its strings cut. "Do you know what was done to me? All because of you."

Kai seemed lost for words. He opened and shut his mouth and then stared at the floor. "L, it wasn't--"

"Phoenix, put me down please."

Phoenix did as he was told and finally took a proper look at Kai. Long surfer hair adorned his head and came just past his ears. A necklace of beads hugged his throat, and a matching set hung from his wrist. Laughter lines creased his face and even in that moment he still managed to hold a carefree attitude that showed Phoenix how little things troubled him. Maybe he was just naive. Maybe he couldn't imagine what horrors his sister had faced. Phoenix had a good idea what had happened to L while she was in prison.

He wasn't sure, but he had guessed. He just never had the courage to ask.

Phoenix walked towards Kai, sure of foot, with anger rolling off him in waves. "Do you know where your sister was?" Phoenix asked, jabbing Kai in the chest.

"She had to do some time in Dredar because of some unforeseen circumstances--"

"Unforeseen circumstances?" said Phoenix.

"Well, L got in trouble with the law, but I was told that she would be taken care of. She wouldn't be doing any hard time and would be out as soon as I knew it. I was guessing that's why she is here today. If she really had been made to do her full sentence, it would still be years before I saw her. Life works in wonderful ways. I never thought any trouble would befall her. If you trust in Soul everything will be okay."

"You religious hippie fool. Is that the right word, Phoenix, hippie?" L demanded.

Phoenix gave her a small nod.

"I got in trouble with the law, did I? I was trying to save your ass from certain gang leaders that you owed money to. I was trying to bring all of them down, to save you from having to pay them credits you didn't have. I went undercover for the law enforcement agency but got set up by both sides. Did you think I was away having a wonderful time?"

"I was told that you would be taken care of. No harm would come to you. What you did was off your own back. No--"

"I was beaten."

"I was told you wouldn't be hurt--"

"I was touched."

"I was told--"

"I was hurt."

"I... I... It shouldn't have happened like that. It shouldn't have... I made a deal. I made a deal," Kai pleaded.

"A deal with who?" said Phoenix.

"Duke," said Kai.

"Did someone say my name?" A man surrounded by thugs walked into the room.

24

In walked the shortest, angriest, meanest-looking thug that Phoenix had ever seen. He wore an open-button shirt that showed tattooed flesh and a well-muscled physique. The tattoos on his hands tried to cover the scars that ran along his knuckles but failed. He walked into the middle of the room and took centre stage.

"What have we here, then?" he asked.

Phoenix looked to his left. A door that could lead to anywhere was being blocked by two goons. He looked to his right. Thick clouded glass covered a whole wall. He tried to see what was beyond it, but it was impossible to tell.

That left only one option.

Phoenix took a casual look over his shoulder at L, and saw that clear glass gave a view of the outside world. The drop wasn't that high–maybe ten feet at most. But yet again, more men lined the back of the room, arms folded over muscled chests. Phoenix gave one a quick smile, but all he got back was a snarl as the thug's Mohawk turned red.

He turned his head back to the Tingoneese who

appeared to be the leader of this little group. "Duke, I would presume," said Phoenix.

"You would *presume* right."

"Funny, I thought you would be taller."

Duke's face twitched slightly, but the rage that flashed across his face was gone as quick as lightning on a stormy night. Duke passed his hand over his shaven head and brought it back to brush off his sleeves. He looked back up to Phoenix with a smile that didn't reach his eyes.

"That little earring of yours reminds me of the sex slave workers that work in the less fortunate part of town. They do anything for a credit or two. They work that pole like their lives depend on it. Well, I guess it does," Duke said with a little chuckle.

"*Less* fortunate parts of town? Since being in this city I haven't seen anything that I would class as privileged. Seems like your stranglehold on the city has brought it to its knees."

"That's where I like everything to be," Duke said with a lewd wink. "But you still haven't answered my question."

"I didn't know you asked one."

"What are you doing here?"

"We came for a little chat with Kai, over here. To sort some things out. Things got a little heated. You know how it is with siblings–one minute hugging, the next throwing bones. Always the same," said Phoenix.

"I know. I had a brother and sister that would constantly get on my nerves when I was younger. Always taking my stuff, always making fun of my height. Putting things just out of reach. They used to call me Little Dukey."

"Children can be so cruel, can't they? How did you ever get over it?"

"I killed them both. Strangled them with my bare hands. Sweetest memory from my childhood."

Phoenix felt his face pull taut and his hands clench. So this was who he was dealing with.

"Something wrong?" asked Duke.

Phoenix could think of nothing better to do than put this sick dog down. The smirk on Duke's face turned his stomach. Phoenix could feel the bile rising in the back of his throat. He wanted nothing more than to spit it in Duke's face. Phoenix forced a smile to his lips.

"Sounds like an interesting story," said Phoenix.

"I will tell you the whole tale, sometime. It makes for wonderful dinner conversation."

"I bet."

"But for now I think there are a few things that we need to discuss--"

"Such as?" said Phoenix.

"For one, the wounding of two of my men," Duke said with a cold stare.

Phoenix scratched the top of his head and looked at a loss. He turned to L, his eyebrows furrowed, and give a shrug. "I injured one of your men. Hmm." Phoenix tapped his lips as his forehead winkled deep in thought. "Can't say I recall doing that."

"Really? Interesting. I had many eyewitness reports that claimed a man of your description blew a leg off one of my men. How did they describe you now... Yes, that was it. So fucking ugly he appeared to be something a dust worm shat out. He was as dark as a dust worm's shit left out on a hot summer's day. With such vivid descriptions matching *your* image, you can see how one would get confused," said Duke.

"Hmm, doesn't sound like me at all. You must be confused," said Phoenix.

"I don't get confused," snarled Duke.

Phoenix gave Duke a dismissive shrug and turned to L. "You got everything you need?"

L nodded her head quickly, hugging her arms across her chest.

"You planning on going somewhere?" Duke asked.

"Right out that door," Phoenix said, pointing to the door behind Duke.

Duke allowed a sly smile to creep along his lips. Shaking his head, he said, "That I can't allow."

"Really? I didn't think the choice was yours to make."

"Now, you see, that's where you're wrong. Everything that happens in this city happens because I allow it to happen. I allow the ships to come and go. I allow the sex workers to work where I choose. I allow the players at my VRG clubs to win and lose as I see fit. So, you see, in regards to you coming and going, that choice was never yours to make."

"Ahh. So you're the law around these parts, then, are you?"

"You could say that," said Duke.

"You see, that's where I have a problem. I was never good at obeying the law when I was growing up. It always left a bitter taste in my mouth. I was something of a wayward child. And you know something... I haven't really changed much," Phoenix said with a shrug.

"Maybe it's about time someone taught you a lesson," Duke said, cracking his knuckles.

"Ahh, poor Dukey. Many have tried, all have failed. What can I say? I am a hard-headed fool."

"Hard heads can be broken--"

Whatever else was meant to be said was swallowed as an explosion blew the door from its hinges. It flew forward and smashed into Duke, lifting him off his feet. Phoenix turned on his heel and pulled L and Kai down. He didn't know why he did it, but his gut had never been wrong before, and he wasn't going to start doubting it now.

Phoenix just had time to cover his head before the glass wall blew outwards, showering shattered glass everywhere. Cries of pain could be heard as glass shards embedded themselves in flesh. Smoke began to fill the room, reducing visibility to zero. Phoenix didn't need to see. He knew which direction he needed to head in. Picking up what he prayed was L and Kai, he ran forward and crashed through the window.

He heard screams as his body became dead weight and dropped like a stone.

25

Air rushed past Phoenix's face as he made his descent. He held L close under one arm. He wanted her close. Safe. Protected. Kai, on the other hand, didn't receive any such treatment. Phoenix had simply thrown him through the window and hoped for the best, expecting the worst. Landing on the balls of his feet, Phoenix expected a bigger jolt than the one he received.

Strange. That should have hurt a lot more than it did.

Phoenix placed L on her feet, and shouts from above him made him look up. Angry bleeding faces could be seen peering down at him. Bringing his pistol to bear he fired a volley of shots up at the window, and the onlookers had the sense to fall back inside.

"Come on! Let's get going," said Phoenix.

Plasma fire rained down from the heavens, scorching the earth around them. Pointing his pistol behind him, Phoenix fired blindly, not caring what he hit. Kai lay some way off, holding his sides and moaning in the dirt. A slight trickle of blood ran down the side of his face. Phoenix grabbed him by the scruff of the neck and half dragged, half lifted him to his feet.

Another explosion rocked the building behind them. Flames leapt into the air, dancing with the darkness of the night. Debris pelted the floor around them as parts of the building began to fall upon them like a rain shower.

"Brother, look what you did!" Kai said. "I don't think this is the best thing to do. I mean, Duke's gonna be mad. Real mad. And when he gets mad, people get hurt–like a lot. Maybe it would be best--"

"Shut up and run," Phoenix said, pushing him forward.

Phoenix looked up just in time to see Saoirse fly through the air ahead of them. She flipped and turned as gracefully as any Olympic gymnast. She landed on her hands and did a double back-flip that planted her on her feet.

"So unnecessary," Phoenix said, running towards her.

"I like to put on a show," Saoirse said with a smile.

"Thanks for the help, back there. Fighting my way out of that would have been messy for all parties involved."

"I could tell you needed some help. Sorry I didn't give you any warning," Saoirse said.

"Don't--"

Shouts from ahead of them drew their attention to a group of men clustered outside the guardhouse. The gang member they had taken out earlier was now awake and well and pointing angrily in their direction.

"I'll thank you later, if we get out of this alive," said Phoenix.

The men in front of them didn't hesitate to raise their weapons in their direction, but their actions were too slow as Saoirse threw what appeared to be small round metallic balls their way. All thoughts of shooting Phoenix and the others vanished as they ran for cover.

Phoenix expected an explosion of some sort, but what he got instead was a light display, as blue lights connected together and leapt ten feet into the air. The blue current leapt onto anything metallic and melted it until it was just a puddle of goo on the ground. Phoenix heard cries and screams from gang members as their guns melted into their flesh. The odd smell of burning flesh and melting metal left a strange taste in the back of Phoenix's throat.

"We need to lose them in the city before we head back to Rusty's," said Phoenix.

A scream of rage cut through the night sky behind them. It threatened that pain would be met until pain became the only emotion that they ever remembered; it would show no mercy.

But all it told Phoenix was that they needed to move.

Duke rose from the rubble of the wooden door like a demon from hell. He lifted himself up to a standing position, his eyes narrowed, teeth clenched. Someone offered a hand but he slapped it away. The flames of the building threatened to lap his back. He looked at his hands and noticed that they were shaking. Closing them into fists, he brought them down to his sides.

"Duke! They're getting away!"

He didn't know who the voice belonged to but it sounded faint. As if someone was shouting it from a distance.

"Duke!"

He snapped his head to the left and saw one of his men shouting something. What could possibly be so important?

"Duke!"

What had he been doing before he hit his head? Who was he talking to? A blurry image from a distance grew larger and larger by the second. The outline was hazy. The image was dark. No. No. The person was dark. Skin like the little balls of drugs he gave the sex workers. Why was he so important?

He felt someone tugging on his arm. He looked their way and they backed off.

Why was that face so important?

What was that in his ear? *Argh! I remember now.* Like a sandstorm dropping all it contained in one area, Duke remembered what had happened. He remembered why he was bleeding. But most of all he remembered why he was so angry.

"I want those fuckers found! I want that fucker with the earring in front of my feet. No one is to kill him. He will pray for death before I am finished with him. L and Kai I want back unharmed. They are both too valuable to me. Do you hear me?" Duke said, looking around at his men.

Duke's men ran before the onslaught of his wrath and rage; anyone who was too slow got a kick up the ass or punch to the back of the head.

"And find who the fuck blew up my warehouse!"

26

Phoenix ducked and dodged as men spilled out of the warehouse like ants. He fired back wildly, trying to give himself as much hope of survival as he could. He didn't dare look back. He heard the shouts and the howling but his single focus was on the streets and alleyways up ahead.

Bricks exploded above his head showering him with mortar.

Saoirse spun around and pointed her gun in his direction. Phoenix's body reacted before he had time to think. He dropped to the ground and plasma bolts singed the fabric of his clothes as they passed overhead. The screams of the dying sounded a lot closer than Phoenix would have liked.

He picked himself back up and ran alongside Saoirse. He didn't say anything but gave her a sideways look and just shook his head.

"What?" she asked.

"Maybe saying 'duck' wouldn't hurt next time," Phoenix said, eyebrows raised.

"There wasn't any time. You're a smart boy, you would have figured it out."

"Sometimes I worry more about you killing me than I--"

The roar of multiple engines brought a halt to what Phoenix was going to say.

L looked over at them wide-eyed.

Kai huffed and puffed next to her, holding his side. He seemed to be in some pain. Phoenix didn't know if it was just because he was unfit or if the fall from the window had done some damage.

"We need to split up," said Phoenix.

"I agree," said Saoirse.

"You take L. I'll take Kai. We meet back at Rusty's."

"No, Phoenix, I'm not leaving my brother again. I can't, I won't. I--"

"L, we don't have a choice! The bigger the group, the easier the target. This is our only option. I'm sorry--"

"You don't understand, Phoenix. You don't understand. I can't leave him. I made a promise," L shouted.

"L, everything will be alright. Trust me. Everything will be okay. Now you need to go with Saoirse, and we'll see you soon. Saoirse, you okay?"

Saoirse looked over her shoulder at the scene behind her. Her face didn't paint a pretty picture of what she saw. Phoenix turned his head to see what had her so worried. Four vehicles that looked liked pickup trucks hovering above the ground dropped the bottom out of his stomach.

"Shit! Hover cars? Really? Fucking hover cars! Do you know how long Earth has been waiting to see one of those invented? I can't believe this shitty-ass planet got there before us. Man, I feel depressed."

"Take to the roofs. Those models are old and can only hover ten feet at most," said Saoirse.

"Be safe!" said Phoenix.

Saoirse gave Phoenix a nod as she dragged L away. They took a sharp left, vanishing from sight. Phoenix fired behind him hoping to draw as much attention his way as possible, so the other two had a chance.

He looked over at Kai, who looked worse than ever. Sweat poured down his red blotchy face, and his hair had taken on a grey tint. The roar of engines kicking into drive pounded in Phoenix's ears.

The enemy was coming.

Phoenix grabbed Kai by the shoulder and pushed him forward. The sounds of hooting and war-cries were too close for Phoenix's liking. He stole a glance behind him and saw a vehicle closing in. It was about the size of a small family car with the roof cut off, and its headlights dazzled Phoenix's vision. He could just about make out men leaning out of the hover car, banging weapons against its sides.

It was closing in. Its lights illuminated everything in front of them. Plasma bolts scorched the earth behind their feet. The noise of the engines drowned out all other sounds.

"Down there," said Phoenix.

They squeezed into a tight alleyway just as the hover car smashed into the wall behind them. The space was too small for it to fit through.

Phoenix pushed Kai forward and looked over his shoulder as an ugly-faced man tried to make his way through the gap. Phoenix fired his pistol and got the satisfying sight of the pursuer holding what was left of his face. The scream that followed warned others of what was to come if anyone dared enter.

"Move, move!" said Phoenix.

"Where do you want me to go?" Kai asked.

"Up that ladder. We haven't got much time."

Kai wheezed and huffed as he pulled his skinny frame up the ladder. Phoenix placed a hand under Kai's ass and pushed him up. Even with Phoenix's support, the going was slow.

"I see you VRG players get a lot of exercise," said Phoenix.

"Listen, man, my brain gets all the exercise it needs. From the prayers that I offer Soul, to the playing of DD4. The mental strain that things like that put you under are like no other. After you have been shown the true signs of the way of the universe, exercise seems so unimportant. You can't--"

"Shut up and move faster. I can't push your ass up this ladder all day."

Kai collapsed as they made it onto the roof of a building. Phoenix pulled himself up and over the edge, and was about to berate Kai when a blow across his shoulders sent him sprawling to his knees.

Phoenix kicked his leg out behind him, making contact with something soft. He climbed to his feet and spun around to see his attacker cupping the spot between his legs.

"Looks like balls are in the same spot the universe over. Too bad for you." Phoenix sent the man flying off the roof with a forward kick to his chest. He ran to the opposite side of the building and saw the tattooed faces of men making their way up another service ladder. They hadn't seen him yet.

Too bad for them.

"Hello, boys, how you doing?"

Three faces looked up at him angrily, the anger quickly turning to fear when Phoenix aimed his pistol down. He picked his shots well. He shot the first goon on the ladder, who collapsed downward on the other two. He listened to their screams of terror all the way down till he heard a thud.

Phoenix ran back to Kai, who was bent over with his hands on his knees. His sweaty face grimaced as Phoenix approached.

At least he wasn't still on his back, thought Phoenix. That was something, he supposed.

"Get your ass moving! I told L that I would get you back to her, and I like to keep my promises. Now fucking move."

There was a loud boom and the building shook under them. Kai moved backwards and tripped over his own feet. He was too close to the edge of the building and fell backwards, swinging his arms in front of him, trying to claw at the air.

Phoenix saw him falling before his eyes. Running forward, he leapt and caught Kai with both hands. Phoenix braced his muscles as Kai's weight took its toll.

Thank God the bastard is skinny.

"Kai, you still alive? Otherwise I'll drop your ass! I don't want to be carrying a dead weight!"

"I'm... I'm... Yeah, I'm still alive."

"Good to hear it. Now, up you come."

For the second time in as many minutes, Kai was once again huffing and puffing, face stricken and hair colourless, on the building roof.

"Stay low. I'm going to see what that was." Phoenix stayed low as he made his way to the other side of the building. He could see men shouting at one another. He couldn't tell what they were arguing over and he didn't care. What caught his attention was a weapon not unlike a cannon sticking out of the boot of the hover car. Phoenix could still see the smoke billowing from the barrel.

"How am I going to... Ah." What appeared to be highly

luminous storage chambers could be seen tucked in the front of the hover car. Phoenix took aim, making sure the shot hit its target. "Surely they wouldn't be so stupid as to..." Phoenix said, pulling the trigger.

The blast from the hover car temporarily blinded Phoenix. The wash of hot air swept over him. There were no screams. There were no cries of pain. The only sound was of roaring flames.

27

Duke paced back and forth. His anger had not burnt out like he thought it would; it had only intensified, the more he reran the night's events. He had been left battered and buried. One eye was swollen and small cuts bled freely. He muttered under his breath as he paced.

Blake got up from where he sat, in a chair off to Duke's side, to see if he could stem the bleeding.

"I told you I'm fine!" Duke said, pushing him away.

Blake's lips pressed into a fine line as he stood in front of Duke. He thrust his hands on his hips and simply shook his head, sitting back down.

"What?" Duke asked.

Blake didn't respond. He simply stared into space.

"Can you believe this? The state they left my warehouse in? My house! Everything is ruined. From the VRG laboratory to the weapons hold. They think this will set me back! Me!"

Duke's pacing increased. He stopped in his tracks and threw a chair across the room. It shattered against the wall.

"Why are you not saying anything? Why do I always have to sort the messes out?"

Blake sat up straight and looked Duke in the eye. He gave Duke a simple flick and wave of his hand before settling back in his chair.

"What do you think I mean? I'm always the one sorting out problems, fixing things, trying to make sure that we live well. You think that's easy?"

Blake shook his head in disbelief and pointed to himself before signing aggressively.

"Oh, so now you didn't ask for this. I see. You remember where we came from? You may forget the cold nights we worked, willing to do anything for anyone's pleasure, but I don't."

Blake stood with such force from where he sat that his chair fell to the floor.

"I remember the nights of tears and pain. I made a promise to you, and I kept it! No one will dare touch us again. No one will dare raise a finger to us again. But all that seems for nothing, from the fucking gratitude I get."

Blake waved and flicked his hands with force. His body was rigid. His jaw was set.

"You just wanted to be free and live happily with me?" Duke said with a bark of laughter. "How long do you think that would have lasted? Where would we have found work? Two ex–pleasure workers. How long do you think it would have been before people tried to take what we had?"

Blake shrugged his shoulders and gave a dismissive wave.

"I'm not being paranoid! You only had to do half the things I had to do. You don't get your hands dirty. You enjoy all the benefits and rewards without doing any of the work.

Life is easy for you, Blake! The deal was for you to look after me and I would look after you!"

Blake began to move his hands but was shouted down.

"Don't interrupt! That's your problem–never wanting to listen. Do you think that fucker with the earring will be the only one hammering at our doors? If we allow them to escape–allow them to win–then all of this is done. And I will not go back to where I came from. Not for anyone!"

A simple hand gesture. A simple question.

"I'll tell you what we're going to do. We're going to get Kai back and lock him up for the rest of his life. Then we're going to get that sister of his and have her show us how to get into that ship of hers."

Blake pointed to Duke, then himself, giving a short sign. His face was emotionless, as he tried to hide the torrent of emotion that ran under the surface.

"What do you mean, then what? Then we continue as we always have."

Blake started to walk away and didn't turn around when his name was shouted. There was no point. He had once loved the person who stood across from him, but now? Things were beginning to change. He just had to decide if he was willing to make his own changes to survive.

28

Phoenix and Kai ran along the rooftops, ducking plasma fire, to the shouts and cries of thugs who had seen their prize in sight.

"Why the fuck are they firing? I thought they would want you alive," said Phoenix.

"They aren't that smart. They haven't embraced the wonders of Soul in their hearts. They're still trapped in their rage instead of addressing it. Peace and happiness is the only true way to live," said Kai.

Phoenix looked at Kai with one raised eyebrow but kept what he was going to say to himself. He would address that hippie shit later. Right now, he needed to keep focused.

A head popped up over the lip of the building in front of them. Phoenix blasted it into oblivion and kept running. They jumped over the gap between the two buildings. Plasma bolts shot up from the ground below. Landing on the opposite roof, they rolled and kept on running.

Kai had seemed to catch his second wind, but Phoenix didn't know how long that would last. They needed to lose the second hover car that followed them. It seemed the four vehicles had split up–two after Phoenix and Kai, and two after Saoirse and L.

Phoenix just hoped the other two were okay.

At the sound of another resounding boom, Phoenix looked over his shoulder. The building was crumbling behind him, falling away. Kai peered over his shoulder and looked back at Phoenix, eyes wide and mouth agape. He didn't say a word. He didn't need to.

"Move!" said Phoenix.

They leapt from one building to the next without stopping, without caring what came next. They just needed to make sure they weren't around for what was to come.

Phoenix felt the roof shake under his feet with the sound of the third boom. He could see his escape in the distance, but his footing was unsure. He *had* to make it.

Phoenix ducked and dived to avoid a plasma bolt. He leapt from one building to the next. Back on his feet, he heard a yell of shock behind him. Kai was wrapped up in what appeared to be a net. Phoenix could see his features mashed against the netting. His face was fearful but he struggled, hopeful that he might still be able to escape.

The net appeared to be attached to an elastic rope, which was pulled taunt against its struggling prey. Kai tried his hardest to crawl free of his entrapment, but Phoenix knew that he didn't have enough time or strength to free himself. As the elastic snapped back it pulled Kai off the roof and into the unknown.

Phoenix knew that the whole event hadn't lasted longer than ten seconds but it felt like a lifetime. He realised too late that he had been standing stationary for far too long.

The final boom brought him from his thoughts. Phoenix's stomach dropped as he felt the roof give way below him. He saw his salvation on the opposite building;

its roof–and safety–was only a hop and a leap away. He pumped his legs but it was of no use. Phoenix saw the beautiful night skyline, where old met new, and marvelled at the beauty of it. He should have taken more time to study it before it was too late.

But none of that mattered as a deafening roar filled his ears and he dropped into the darkness below.

L, Saoirse and Freyan sat quietly in a corner of Rusty's. L tapped her fingers along the tabletop and flicked her gaze behind her every so often. The door to the inn had not opened for a good while, but she still hoped that Phoenix and Kai would walk through the door at any minute.

She hugged her arms around herself, as her hair changed from one shade to the next. The fire crackling in the pit kept the chill night air at bay but she still couldn't help but shudder. Running her hands up and down her arms, she let out a small sigh.

She took another look over her shoulder.

Nothing.

Where the sands are they?

She had thought that coming back home would bring all her old memories of the place back, but the longer she stayed there, the more she wanted to leave. She had romanticised the places she knew and the people that lived, breathed, worked in the city. Now she realised it was just all a dream.

The streets were nothing more than dirt tracks and the buildings just shaky bits of metal stuck together. The people were husks with the life sucked out of them.

This planet had that effect on people. It *wanted* to break

them. The days were too hot to do anything but seek shade and the nights too cold to do anything but wrap up near a fire and sleep.

L knew she shouldn't be angry at the Tingoneese. They were her people. They had endured global disaster, world wars, civil wars and everything in between. But through it all, her people didn't seem to want to...better themselves. They allowed one evil dictator after the next to lead the way.

Before Duke had run the city, there had been someone else just as bad. No doubt the person after Duke wouldn't be any better. It was almost as though her people enjoyed being repressed.

Her time in Dredar had made her forget the reality of her life back home. Or maybe she had just wanted to gloss it over and pretend her life there would have been better than being shut away in some cage.

When she had been in that jail cell, she had wanted to be anywhere else–be a *slave* anywhere else. She had thought she would never see the light of day again. The end of the line. The only way out was through death.

But then she had met Midnight. Midnight had given L hope. She had given L a reason to dream again–a reason to dream of somewhere better. Somewhere happier. L had hoped she would find it with this newly formed crew. She only hoped and prayed that she could take her brother along for the ride too.

L looked over her shoulder once more and saw Phoenix standing in the doorway.

He was alone.

29

Duke paced up and down his office. The charred carpet and a hole the size of a hover vehicle in one of the walls was a constant reminder of the earlier blast. The cold wind gusting through the hole did nothing to cool his temper.

He couldn't contain it. It consumed him.

"Blake! Blake!"

He waited for a response but got no answer.

"Where in the sands is he? He's never around when I need him."

Duke stopped in front of the remains of what had once been his desk and stabbed his finger on a button that connected him to the warehouse holocoms. It beeped and beeped, waiting for someone–anyone–to answer it.

"Hello?" a voice on the other end finally said.

"Where is everyone?"

"They appear to be still out, sir. You did say for everyone to make Kai and L a priority."

"A priority--"

"It means--"

"I know what it means! I haven't got sand for brains. What is taking them so long? Did they leave on foot? We have hover cars. The job should have been done, already."

"I can only guess, sir, that they ran into some sort of problem," the voice said through the holocom.

"You can only guess, huh? What a fucking load of good you are to me. Inform me when they have arrived," Duke said.

"Anything else, sir?"

"Is... Have... I haven't seen Blake in a while, do you know where he is?"

The only response was the howling of the wind as it came through the hole in the wall. The silence grew, and if Duke wasn't mistaken he could almost hear a gulp at the other end of the line.

"Well, err--"

"Spit it out," said Duke.

"Well, the last time... No, there has been no sign of Blake anywhere. Some of the men said that he told them that he would be back later, but he had bags with him. Packed bags. I can only take a guess at where he would be now, but if he said that he would be back, then I guess he will be."

Duke said nothing but placed both hands on his desk. His head bent low as he closed his eyes to the hot feeling that stirred in his stomach.

So this was what it had come to? This was how it was going to end?

"Sir?"

"Err, report back to me if you see him. Let him know that I would like to speak to him."

"Will do, sir."

Duke resumed his pacing. He didn't want to dwell on the thoughts pushing their way to the surface. He didn't have time to face them, right now. They would only slow him down. They would only make him weaker. For now, he had issues that needed his attention.

Any sign of weakness on his part would be seen as an invitation for someone to challenge him. Then he would be fighting a war on two fronts.

No!

He needed to appear strong. He needed to crush his enemies and spread their ashes to the winds.

The only way he could do that was if he appeared strong, even though his world was crumbling around him.

"Sir?" a voice from the holocom said.

"What?"

"They have captured Kai. He's in the building."

A ghost of a smile graced Duke's lips. "Bring him up to me."

Duke didn't have to wait long to hear the footsteps of his prey making their way towards him. They echoed along the halls that led to his office. He leaned against his desk, arms folded over his chest, eyes half closed, thoughts touching on a million things but never resting for long on one.

A knock on his door made him lift his head. "Enter."

In walked a ragged-looking Kai. Multiple cuts on his face bled freely, his lip was swollen, and one eye was forced shut, already blackening. He shuffled forward, head down, quiet as a mute. His hands were bound in front of him. His clothes appeared torn in some places and had been reduced to strips of material in others.

Two thugs stood on either side of Kai, each holding onto one arm.

"Really, is that any way to treat a friend?" Duke said. "Release him–this is no way to talk about business."

One of the thugs did as he was told and cut the restraints

from Kai's wrists. Kai rubbed where they had bitten into his skin. He rotated his hands around in small circles.

"So," said Duke.

"So," replied Kai.

Silence dominated the room while they stared at each other.

Duke drummed his fingers along the desk behind him. He stared deep into Kai's eyes, waiting for the fool to lower his gaze. But he did not. Something was amiss.

"What seems to be the problem?" Duke asked.

"Nothing. Nothing at all," Kai said sullenly.

Duke's fingers picked up their pace along the desk. His tongue clicked against the roof of his mouth and his brow wrinkled in thought. His eyes narrowed to slits, and he slammed his hands down with force, making everyone in the room jump.

"Come now, Kai, we can't have you all silent and moody when you're always the life of the party. Tell me what seems to be the issue. Tell me how we can both be of help to each other."

Kai folded his arms across his chest and shook his head from side to side. His lips upturned, and Kai shook his head again.

"Come on, Duke, why all the lies? I thought you were a son of Soul. Why go through all this when the veil has been lifted?"

"I don't know what you mean, young Kai," Duke said, forcing a smile to his lips.

"My sister. My blood. You had her falsely imprisoned--"

"Who told you such lies? Your sister is a criminal, through and through. Of course she would say such things. We both know--"

"We both know what? Never to trust the word of a criminal? If that were the case, I would rather trust blood than you, seeing as both of you are in the same boat."

"Look, you fool! I don't know what she told you, but I went to painstaking efforts to see that she didn't pay the full price for her crimes. Do you know how much it cost me?"

"To set her up?" said Kai.

Duke gritted his teeth. His eyes narrowed, and he passed a hand through his hair. "I did everything I could to keep your sister safe. And because of that, we had a deal. You'd work for me, doing as I asked, and I would make sure the law went easy on her. Nothing has changed. Apart from the fact that she has destroyed my warehouse, and injured or killed some of my men. I don't care what she means to you, I can't allow this to go unpunished."

"Listen--"

"No, *you* listen. Nothing has changed. The deal still remains the same. You are indebted to me, and I am not even talking about the credits you still owe because of your VRG habit. So this is what will happen. Everything will go back to normal, and I will smooth this mess over. Is that clear?"

Kai swept his hair out of his eyes and shook his head in disbelief. "Sorry, my brother, that won't fly--"

The backhand Duke delivered spun Kai around and dropped him to the floor. Kai held his cheek where the blow had landed, a red bruise already forming beneath his fingers.

Duke walked towards Kai, who shuffled back on the floor, but his back bumped against the legs of one of the thugs behind him.

Duke squatted down so they were eye to eye. "Listen to me, you VRG fucker. I will break every bone in that worthless body of yours till you do as I say. I will start with the ones that ain't useful to me. The feet. The legs. The ribs. Then I will start chopping bits off. I will continue to do so till I find a replacement to work for me. You think you're a special little sand grain? That no one can do your job?

"You're wrong. And I will have great pleasure inflicting pain on you–showing you just how wrong you are."

Duke stood and straightened his clothes. He looked down his nose at the pitiful thing on the floor. "Do we understand each other?" he said.

30

Phoenix couldn't stand the horrified look L gave him when he walked through the door. She broke down at the sight of him, crying and screaming, while the onlookers of the inn watched the scene with amusement. Hadn't he promised her? Hadn't he given her his word?

But yet here he was, back safe, without any injuries. And where was her brother?

Phoenix had tried to answer her questions but none of his answers placated L. Hell, they didn't even appease him. So while L sobbed and cried on Saoirse's shoulder, Phoenix knocked back a few shots of whatever the hell was put in front of him.

It did nothing to sooth the raging fire burning in the pit of his stomach. If anything, the alcohol was only fuel for the flames.

"So you believe Kai is still..." said Saoirse.

"Yes, I do believe he's alive. They captured him by net. The only reason for that would be to keep him alive. Duke still needs him. Kai is profitable to him. Too profitable to risk hurting him. So he must be safe and sound. The only thing we need to find out is how to get to him. Duke will no doubt have tripled his forces, so trying the same way as last time would be next to impossible," said Phoenix.

"How do...you...know he's alive? I mean, anything could have happened to him," L said through tearful sobs.

"L, trust--" Phoenix stopped himself and scratched his stubble, before letting out a sigh. "Don't trust what I say. Just think what you would do if you were Duke. Why kill the one person that makes you a daily profit? Without Kai, Duke loses control of the VRG store. It would be suicide. He needs those credits to keep a stranglehold on the city.

"No, he won't hurt Kai. But he will come for us. A psychotic prick like that will stop at nothing to make sure that we are dealt with. His reputation demands it. And trust me, he's all about reputation."

"Then what do we do?" L asked.

"I'm still working on that."

"Well, work faster! Now Duke knows I'm back in the city, he will want me to unlock the doors to my ship. The ship I slaved to build. I will not allow him to have it! It means too much to me," said L.

"What's so important about this ship? With Duke's wealth, surely he can purchase any ship he wants," said Freyan.

"My ship is different. It was the prototype. It has flaring twice the speed as the normal standard. Weaponry that could punch a hole through a dreadnought. Shields that can withstand punishment most ships couldn't.

"It was going to be a ship that this planet could manufacture. That would bring credits and jobs to every city on this sand bowl. But before my plans could fully get underway, Duke happened. He wants the ship for himself. He wants to sell the ship's design to the highest bidder."

"So what has stopped him?" said Phoenix.

"It's simple, really. The ship has so much security you'd need a small army just to crack it open. Without me, no one is getting into that baby."

"If what you say is true, L, then this ship could revolutionise space travel. It would take this planet from a class four to a class two overnight. It would make you rich beyond your dreams. As an inventor, I would love to see it," said Freyan.

"That's the thing, Freyan. I don't think I want to put it into production anymore," said L.

"Why?"

"Because the universe is bloody enough without me adding to it. This ship would only make it easier for races to kill one another. It would only make untouched, unspoilt, planets easier to find. I can't have that on my conscience. I...just can't."

"Ah, I see," Freyan said quietly.

"Has anyone seen Plowstow, lately?" asked Phoenix.

The silence that answered the question allowed the wind to carry it away over the sand dunes. Phoenix looked to each face but received blank stares. He let out a small sigh and leaned back in his chair. That was something else he would have to deal with, sooner or later.

"Phoenix, what are we going to do? I can't leave Kai in Duke's clutches. He's the only family I have."

Phoenix saw Saoirse's jaw clench tight and her lips set in a firm line. The lioness was ready for war. Looking to L, Phoenix placed his hand over hers. "Nothing's changed. We will get him back."

Phoenix's head snapped to Saoirse, who had gone rigid. Her eyes were wide. Her nostrils were flared. The tension in her shoulders could crack rocks.

A deadly silence had now filled the inn.

Phoenix followed Saoirse's gaze and saw the person who had set her on edge. A tall, dark-skinned male stood in the centre of the inn. His long red leather trench coat brushed the floor and the tight black top underneath highlighted his well-muscled physique. Braided hair ended with little golden bells on the end of the plaits.

Phoenix's gaze swept the female with green skin and orange hair cut into a short bob next to him. Her curves pulled at something deep inside him. She caught him staring and gave him a wink and a smile that was all canines.

"The Bell Man," said Saoirse in a whisper, that said more than a shout ever could.

31

Phoenix stared at Saoirse for more information but none was forthcoming. Nothing more was uttered. Around the inn, people slowly got up and made their way towards the exits. The bartender's customers left in droves, and he himself was nowhere to be seen. It seemed that he knew something that Phoenix didn't.

Not everyone left. A handful of men began to spread themselves out around the room, each taking a spot near an exit or window.

Huh. So this is how the game is going to be played. Then let us play it well.

"So, do you have a name, *Bell Man?*" asked Phoenix.

"Names are such...miserable things. They label someone for life. They bind you to their will. They chain you so you can never be someone different. Never be someone more."

Phoenix rolled his eyes, "I could always call you Dick-head, or Fuckface, or Shitface or--"

"Rustem! The name is Rustem."

"Ah, so, you see, you do have a name. That wasn't that hard, was it?"

"Manners, Phoenix Jones, are something I see you lack. Manners tend to go a long way in not getting you killed."

"Well, as you can clearly see by my perky condition, I have done quite well so far. So, tell me, how do you know my name?"

A small chuckle escaped Rustem's lips. He shook his head and the bells made a beautiful medley. "Ahh, Mr Jones, your name echoes among the stars. The man from Earth imprisoned for a crime he didn't know he committed. A prisoner facing life in Dredar escapes from the clutches of death. Your name is growing in weight with each passing day.

"What shall your next adventure be? What shall the next chapter in your story read?"

"That I was handsome. That I made women across the stars faint at my name. That I was dashing, in victory and defeat. You know, not much, just enough to warm me in my old age. Anyway, you seem to know who I am, but I don't know who you are."

"I already told you. My name is Rustem. What else is there to say?"

Phoenix let out an exaggerated sigh before turning to Saoirse. "Who is this fool?"

Saoirse's hands were placed on both her blades. She didn't appear to hear Phoenix. Her expression still hadn't changed.

"Saoirse," Phoenix said.

"If I am the demon pirate hunter, then he is the devil. He is the thing everyone fears. He is a killer for hire, only called when the caller wants just one outcome–death."

"I see," said Phoenix.

"He has never lost a kill," said Saoirse.

"And who is she?" Phoenix asked, nodding to the female next to Rustem.

"She is none of your concern," said Rustem.

Phoenix nodded his head and a small smile graced his lips. "I already know the answer to this question--"

"Then why ask it?" said Rustem.

"Who sent you?"

"Now, we both know the answer to that, don't we?" said Rustem.

"I guess we do," Phoenix said, launching the table in front of him into the air and bringing his pistol to bear.

Phoenix fired at any target in front of him. He didn't care who he hit, he just wanted to create as much chaos as possible. Rustem and the green female ducked for cover as plasma bolts sailed over their heads.

Saoirse grabbed L by the front of her clothes with one hand and hauled her over the bar counter. Glasses and bottles shattered as she made impact on the other side.

"L, you okay?" said Phoenix.

"Couldn't be better. Just have glass up my ass, but you know."

"That's my girl," said Phoenix.

Phoenix ducked as return fire came his way. They had to make it out of here alive. He hadn't travelled across the stars just to die here, in some dirty, flea-ridden bar.

"Rustem, old buddy, old pal. Can't we talk this out? Like the fine gentlemen we are?" Phoenix said, peering over the table and chairs.

"Now, Mr Jones, why would I want to do that? Your defeat is all but assured," said Rustem.

"I don't know. We could talk--" Phoenix saw one of Rustem's men pop his head up. Phoenix didn't hesitate and blew the top of his head clean off. The remains splattered behind the man. Gelatinous red substance slowly slid down the wall.

"We could talk about how we both look slightly alike–me being better-looking, of course–and how we don't come from the same planet. I would love to know what your world is like."

"It is not that much different from yours," said Rustem.

A lull amidst the chaos descended.

"That's right, Mr Jones. I have been to Earth. What wonders I saw. What knowledge I gained," said Rustem.

Images of the twins flashed before Phoenix's eyes.

"Don't worry, Mr Jones. I didn't leave with bloody hands."

Phoenix's chest rose and fell. He gripped his pistol tighter. Rage coloured his vision. He couldn't hear anything around him. He couldn't see. Then, like the passing of a storm, he felt an arm on his shoulder and the clouds parted. Phoenix looked over and saw Freyan, who gave him a slight nod.

A head popped up to the left, but Phoenix wasn't quick enough. Saoirse's hand flew past his ear, releasing a throwing knife. The blade sank into the enemy's eye, hilt deep.

"Bloody hands? Looks like you'll be leaving with no men, at this rate!" said Phoenix.

Two bodies rose from their hiding spots and began to rain fire upon their location. Bits of wood melted and bubbled from the plasma onslaught.

"We can't stay here all day," Phoenix whispered over his shoulder.

"On my mark. We shall make a move," said Saoirse.

"What about L?" said Phoenix.

"She will know what to do," said Saoirse.

Phoenix could hear rustling behind him, as Saoirse began preparing God knew what. The men were slowly walking their way. Their plan was simply to walk the crew down, laying down continuous fire. Simple but effective.

A pistol appeared over Phoenix's shoulder. He had one already, but it seemed that Saoirse wanted him to fire both. He guessed the job of returning fire, while the group escaped, was all on him.

"Now!" said Saoirse.

Phoenix brought the pistols up and over the table and held his fingers on the triggers. A battle-cry erupted from his lips. Fire erupted from the barrels and made its way towards their attackers. One had the sense to dive out of the way, but the other wasn't so smart. Plasma fire met plasma fire and created a beautiful maelstrom ball of energy. Light crackled and flickered, breaking windows and shorting the overhead lights.

It pulsed like it had a heart. It was beautiful to behold. But it was growing bigger and bigger by the second.

Saoirse threw two small balls that left a smoke trail in their wake. They exploded upon impact with the floor. Waves of smoke billowed out of them, filling the inn in seconds.

The ball of energy was still visible among the smoke. It glowed like an ancient artefact, hanging suspended in mid air.

As the others began to move out from their hiding places, Phoenix jumped to his feet and let loose with everything he had. He appeared like a demon amid the mist.

Plasma bolts seemed to explode from his hands as he bellowed his anger at his attackers.

How dare they threaten him! How dare they threaten his crew!

He saw heads lift from where the men crouched, but his shots forced them to duck back down again. Turning on his heels, he began to run towards a window.

The green plasma ball grew larger and larger in his wake.

"Retreat! Retreat!" an unknown female voice screamed behind him.

Phoenix dived through the window just as a green flash of light exploded behind him.

32

Plowstow rounded the corner that would take him to Rusty's. He felt good; things were finally looking up for him. After his deal was made, he would have enough credits to do whatever he wanted. Go wherever he wanted. He would be able to leave this sand bowl behind and jet towards the stars. He allowed a smile to cross his face at the thought.

Would he miss the others?

He stopped in his tracks; he didn't know how to answer that. He had always looked after himself, first and foremost. That was the number one rule to living in this universe. He had seen too many souls who had tried to help or better the masses.

Fools!

He had seen where help and kindness got them–pinned to a wall in some back alley, pockets emptied of credits, jewels and anything else that was valuable.

No, thinking of himself above all others was what had gotten him this far, so why change a habit of a lifetime?

But, if it wasn't for the help of the others you would still be in Dredar, said a little voice.

If it wasn't for my so-called friends I wouldn't be in there in the first place, shouted a larger voice.

Plowstow shook his head and continued on walking. He didn't have to make a choice *right now*, did he? He had enough time to decide what to do later.

First, he would enjoy spending some of his credits on the pleasures that this planet had to offer, and then he could plan his future.

Plowstow came to a halt, staring at Rusty's. He saw the unmistakeable plasma bolts zipping back and forth inside as shots were fired. Plowstow ran and ducked behind a stack of barrels and held his breath.

Should he rush in and help? Was it even Phoenix and the others that were in danger? He could be running into a fight that had nothing to do with him whatsoever. He could be risking his life for nothing.

An unmistakeable small figure burst forth from the inn doors and made a run towards the darkness.

L! As the ship's engineer ran for all she was worth, Plowstow debated whether he should follow L or not. No. She knew these streets better than he did. She would be okay.

Plowstow got up from where he crouched and was making his way towards the inn when the sound of breaking windows echoed through the air. Saoirse and Freyan erupted from a window. They both landed and rolled, running in the same direction as L.

That only left Phoenix. Had he been injured?

Plowstow crept forward in the darkness, thinking the battle was over, but Phoenix emerged from the inn like a demon from the planet Trag. The inn's windows exploded behind him, and Plowstow dropped to the ground. He lay there, hands over his head, waiting. Listening. Lifting his head up, he looked for Phoenix but saw no sign of him.

Instead, Odessa emerged from the inn with the Bell Man. The bells in his hair caught the moonlight and flashed in the night. Plowstow swallowed. The credits–and all the dreams that came with them–vanished in a puff of smoke.

33

Duke sat behind his desk, frowning, as he stared at the month's figures. They would be short again. This business wasn't his dream; it wasn't even his passion. When he and Blake were first coming up, they needed credits, and petty crime paid well. Nothing too complicated. Nothing that would put them at much risk. Intimidate a club owner here, threaten a storekeeper there. If words didn't get the message across, then he would have to resort to something more painful.

The work was easy, and he found the more he did it, the more he liked causing pain instead of being on the receiving end of it. It wasn't Blake's sort of thing. He always came up with the ideas, while Duke was the muscle who liked the heavy-handed approach.

One job led to another, and they started to rise up the crime ladder. It wasn't hard. Most of their colleagues where dimwitted fools who had more sand between their ears than brains.

It had been simple–easy. Then, one day, Duke was the

leader, with Blake in the shadows. Blake was his rock, his left hand that held the right back when words were needed instead of violence. But after a while, the responsibilities of life started to create a wedge between them.

Blake thought every problem could be talked through, while Duke knew the truth. Those lowlife worm eaters that walked the street didn't know the meaning behind being diplomatic. Force was the only thing they understood.

Force and violence.

Then the arguments started. Small ones at first, nothing major; nothing that couldn't be sorted with a gift and a smile. But then the fights between them got bigger and nastier, and nothing Duke did or said could smooth it over. No gift was enough, no sweet whispers cooled the flames that roared and smouldered.

Now he was there alone, staring at numbers that didn't add up. How could they be losing so many credits?

The payments to the law and certain Council members had increased year by year. The ways that he hid his credit from other crime lords were always closely monitored. It all amounted to problems that he shouldn't have. It was as if his operation had turned into a corporation, with all the risks and none of the rewards.

Duke threw the papers in front of him across the room. Shouts from the floors below him drew him to the present.

What is it now?

The sound of an explosion startled him.

What the-

The shouts turned to screams and plasma fire echoed around his warehouse.

Boom!

Another explosion shook the floor beneath Duke's feet.

He grabbed the desk and righted himself. He walked over to the weapons that lined his walls and grabbed a bolt-action rifle. Bigger, meaner, and with a kickback that could dislocate a shoulder, the bolt-action rifle was only meant for one thing. Leaving big fucking holes in anything that moved.

Another ear-splitting scream filled the air. The dark glass that gave Duke privacy shattered as a body flew through it. It landed in a splatter of blood, glass and body parts.

Duke recognised the face; it was one of his men.

An unknown face appeared in the space where the glass used to be. Duke pulled the trigger and blasted the head clean off its shoulders.

"In my own fucking warehouse! You fuckers dare–dare!–to attack me?"

Rage coursed through his veins like magma. Duke kicked his office door off its hinges and blasted another body backwards. It landed in a messy heap metres away. Walking down his corridors, he saw signs of the battle raging inside his walls. Duke rounded a corner and a hand holding a plasma sword descended towards his face. Dropping to the floor he landed heavily on his back, but his trigger was pulled before his back made contact with the floor.

The force of the bolt punched his attacker in the stomach, lifting him off his feet. He slammed against the ceiling and back to the floor with a wet slap.

Duke got to his feet, breathing heavily. He made his way towards where the shouts were loudest. On the stairway, he stared down at the scene below.

A circle of his men surrounded a group of what appeared to be the attackers.

Centre stage, dark features emotionless, with bells chiming with every movement his head made, was none other than Rustem.

"Ah, finally–our good host shows himself. We have a great deal to talk about," Rustem said with a smile.

34

Duke stood still as he surveyed the scene below him. His warehouse was in chaos and disarray. Bodies of his men and Rustem's littered the floor. Broken glass and furniture added to the mix.

Rustem stood with a group of men, all with weapons drawn. None wavered as they pointed them at Duke's men. These were professionals.

From his vantage point, Duke looked down his nose and crossed his arms over his chest. "Why are you here, Rustem?"

"I thought I would make a social call. See how things have been. I can see this wonderful planet has lost none of its charm," said Rustem.

"Indeed it hasn't. I must show you how hungry the worms can get. The big ones can swallow some ships whole."

"Is that so? Wonderful creatures. Just wonderful. The more time I spend travelling this vast universe, the more I am amazed at what it has to offer. So many planets to see, so little time. It really takes the breath away. For instance, do you know that on a planet called Earth, they eat something called ice cream? It's frozen and comes in different flavours. Wonderful stuff, that--"

"Earth! Now how can one little planet be getting so much attention?" said Duke.

"Oh, does the name ring a bell?"

Duke rolled his eyes and tapped his fingers along the railing. "I may have heard it in passing. But what is it that you want, Rustem?"

"I believe we can help each other."

"Do you now? Help! Is this what you call help?" Duke gestured to the mass of bodies. "Killing my men? Acting like you're the law? I know that many believe you're some sort of creature that lurks in the night. That your name should only be uttered in a whisper, lest you appear. That you can't be killed.

"Well, shall we put that theory to the test?"

"Killing me now shall accomplish none of your goals," Rustem said.

"But I shall enjoy it very much."

"In my experience, pleasure that one waits for is always better than pleasure gained instantly. Duke, the crime lord of a sand castle. The slave who made something more of himself. The people who chained and whipped him are now at his mercy. How does it feel to hold the whip, instead of being threatened by it?"

"Feels heavy."

"I am sure it must," said Rustem.

"But enough of this. You've still not told me how you can help me. From where I am standing, you need my help. This is my city. These are my people. Nothing happens unless I say so," said Duke.

"And yet you didn't know I was here," Rustem said with a smile.

Duke bit back the rage boiling in his throat and gripped his rifle till his knuckles glowed white. He knew Rustem's reputation. This creature wouldn't be standing in front of him unless he wanted something important. Or someone had hired him to get something they couldn't get themselves.

"I am still waiting for an answer," said Duke.

"There is someone important that I need from this city. Someone that I believe you have had a run-in with--"

"And who would that be?"

"Oh, no one of great value, I assure you. A simple man from a planet called Earth. How a single unknowing event, like an attack on someone important, can cause such a chain reaction is beyond me. His actions have such far-reaching consequences I shudder to think what will happen if he continues to roam free," said Rustem.

"And this Earth man would be?"

"Phoenix Jones. He wears a distinctive earring. Almost garish, one might say."

"One might, might they?" said Duke.

The heaviness of the silence that descended made everyone nervous. People on both sides kept their hands glued to their triggers, their gazes sweeping from Rustem to Duke. Blood had been shed and was ready to gush forth again unless some sort of agreement was reached.

"I am sorry, Rustem, but that worm eater is mine. Now I know his name, it will bring me even more pleasure to drive my fist down his throat."

"I know you believe you have a claim on him, like the stars have a claim on the darkness in space, but he offended someone before you. His life has already been claimed. It was already written, so it must be done," said Rustem.

"As I see it, if I kill you, and everyone you brought to my warehouse, then there will be no one to stand in my way."

As the last words fell from Duke's mouth the tension rose like a swell of the ocean. Jaws clenched. Grips tightened. Muscles flexed.

"Steady, steady, steady. If you go down this path you will lose something you have been after since the dawn of time. Something special to only you. Something that only you and I know the value of. Knowledge that has been out of your reach for some time," said Rustem.

"Which is?"

"I have the girl, L, and all the knowledge she holds. Now, shall we discuss the matter of Phoenix Jones?"

35

Phoenix, Saoirse and Freyan sat in a room just about big enough to swing a cat in above a shop of some sort. The owner hadn't been willing to take any amount of credits for the room Saoirse had acquired. It seemed that Phoenix's image, along with the rest of the crew, had been blasted city-wide by Duke. A reward was being offered for any information that would lead to their capture.

The owner had turned white as a sheet upon seeing their faces, his hair going the same colour. He shook his head furiously, saying he wanted no trouble. Saoirse had draped her arm over his shoulder and whispered something that Phoenix couldn't quite hear in his ear. Whatever was said seemed to do the trick, as they were shown to the room they now occupied.

Saoirse paced back and forth like a caged lioness. "She should be here, by now. I sent a message about where we are to everyone's holocom. This makes no sense."

Phoenix had an unsettled feeling in the pit of his stomach. He couldn't shake it, no matter how hard he tried; something didn't feel right.

"I'm sure she will be along shortly," said Freyan.

Saoirse either didn't hear or chose not to, as her pacing didn't stop. "I should have... There must be... This isn't--" Saoirse shook her head and passed her hands through her hair.

Footsteps made their way up a flight of stairs towards them. Phoenix and Saoirse grabbed their weapons while the echoes grew closer.

Someone knocked three times.

Phoenix held his finger to his lips and moved towards the door. Only one shadow blocked the light from outside. Only one that he could see, anyway.

"Who is it?" he asked in a gruff voice.

The silence on the other side only lasted a heartbeat. "Phoenix, is that you? It's Plowstow. Open the door, it's crazy out there."

Phoenix gave a nod to Saoirse, who hid behind the door, pistol and knife at the ready. Phoenix opened the door a crack and saw that Plowstow was indeed alone. He swept into the room in a whirlwind of panic.

Phoenix poked his head out the door and checked the hallway. The coast was clear, but he still couldn't shake the feeling in the pit of his stomach.

Saoirse pointed her pistol at the back of Plowstow's head. He raised both his trembling hands in the air, his eyes wide in panic.

"What's this about? Come on, I thought we are all on the same team here. Don't...do anything crazy," said Plowstow.

"Where were you?" Saoirse asked through gritted teeth.

"Nowhere."

"Nowhere? I didn't know such a place existed," said Phoenix.

"Come on, y'all. You *know* me. It's me," said Plowstow, licking his lips.

"I will not ask again. Where were you? If I do not like the answer, I will blow your brains out the front of your head," said Saoirse.

Plowstow's eyes darted back and forth. Beads of sweat trickled down his forehead and his chest rose and fell. One hand went to wipe his forehead, but stopped midway. His tongue clicked against his canines and he swallowed. "I went for a walk, to try and cool off. My feelings were mighty hurt after our last conversation--"

Freyan snorted and Plowstow narrowed his eyes in Freyan's direction.

"Truth be told, I was looking for any ship off this rock. I didn't want to stay here a minute longer than necessary. This place doesn't sit well with me–it's the heat. It doesn't do my skin a lick of good. So I searched and searched for a ship–any ship–but there was nothing that took my fancy--"

"No one wanted you, you mean," said Freyan.

"No. There just wasn't a ship that could meet my high standards," said Plowstow.

Freyan shook his head and turned away.

"So, after that, where did you go?" asked Phoenix.

"Boozing and whoring, mostly. Till I ran out of credits."

Phoenix gave a slight nod of the head before letting out a heavy sigh. "Well, while you were enjoying yourself, we went to save L's brother from Duke. I failed. Then we had more trouble at Rusty's–someone called Rustem has decided he wants my head--"

"Rustem! The Rustem? Fuck," said Plowstow.

"Heard of him, then? Well, after he made his appearance, a firefight ensued and we got away. But L hasn't returned," said Phoenix.

"That explains the message I got. I thought it was weird. All it said was 'We have one of your own'. It was from an old contact I used to run with, a female Orcian called Odessa."

The roar that erupted from Saoirse's throat brought dust down from the rafters. It was part pain, part fury. Phoenix saw her hand move and he sped forward, knocking her hand upwards. The pistol she was holding went off in a flash of green light. Phoenix held her hand firm and stared into the pits of fury that were her eyes as bits of the ceiling rained down on their shoulders. He didn't say anything. He didn't need to. He simply gave a small shake of his head.

Saoirse tore her hand from his grip and folded her arms over her chest. Her nostrils flared as she stared defiantly in Phoenix's direction.

"Now, Plowstow, tell me how you are the only one who received this message? Tell me how, out of the rest of us, you got this message? Because to anyone looking in from the outside, it would appear that you are not even part of the crew.

"So please explain to me, carefully, how is it that you–*you*, Plowstow–received such a message," said Phoenix.

"Well...like I said, I once ran with Odessa doing odd jobs. Anything that pays, you know. Nothing major. Then we parted ways. She had a thing for me, but it was only one-way. Since then I heard rumours and news of what she was up to, here and there, but that's it. I swear, Phoenix."

Phoenix said nothing as he stared at the Orcian, his fingers tapping the outside of his leg.

"I did hear she joined forces with Rustem, but I paid it

no mind. I ain't one for snooping. Plus who would be crazy enough to join forces with a monster like that? But it must be true, if she messaged me on his behalf."

"What exactly did the message say?" said Phoenix.

"We have one of your own. Your move."

36

The walls were closing in. Phoenix could feel them. He could brush his fingers against them. They closed off his only view of the setting sun. The walls felt absolute.

"Plowstow, go out and gather as many hover vehicles as you can find. The smaller and faster the better--"

"I don't have any--"

"I don't care if you have no credits. Find a way to get them. Steal them, hold whoever you need to at gunpoint. But let me make this clear, Plowstow, if you come back empty-handed, then I'll be closing you and Saoirse in a small room together for a nice long chat."

Phoenix could see that Plowstow was about to say something else, but Phoenix stared him down. He didn't have time for this: the whining, the complaining, the moaning. It would all stop now.

Plowstow gave him a small nod. "What do you want me to do about the message?"

"Leave it, for now. Don't do anything until I have a plan. I want complete radio silence on our end. If they message again, let me know," said Phoenix.

Plowstow stared at him open-mouthed, about to say something else, but Phoenix shook his head and pointed to the door. Plowstow grunted, turned his back and left.

"Saoirse, get me as many guns as you can. The bigger the better. I want to make some big fucking holes," said Phoenix.

"Phoenix, they have her," Saoirse said in a small voice.

If Phoenix didn't know better, he would have mistaken it for a plea, a cry for help. But looking into the pools of blackness that were Saoirse's eyes made him shudder. God help the people who got in her way when the fighting started. He had never seen such anger. She was almost at breaking point.

"I know. But I need you to do something for me. I need you to hold it together, just for a few more days, at least. Then the fun really starts. Get me what I've asked for, and we shall make anyone who stands in our way pay."

Saoirse gave him a slight nod and made her way out the door, her hair billowing behind her.

Phoenix placed his hands on his head, letting out a deep-rooted sigh.

"Difficult, isn't it?" said Freyan.

"What is?" said Phoenix.

"Being a captain, a leader."

"Is that what you call what I'm doing?" Phoenix said, letting out a snort of laughter.

"What would you call it?"

"Helping some friends in their hour of need. Righting a few wrongs."

"To some, that's what leadership is all about."

"Well...those people are idiots." Phoenix turned his head to look at Freyan. The Bloodless one appeared to be amused; his eggshell-white features smiled faintly. Even in the gloom of the dingy room, Freyan's gold joints shone like lost treasure at the bottom of the ocean.

"After this is done, we should run," said Freyan.

"Run?" Phoenix repeated with a wrinkled brow.

Freyan stretched his arms out behind his head before bringing them down on his lap. The bed he sat on creaked as he shifted his weight. He opened and closed his mouth a few times, seeming to search for the right thing to say. "Phoenix, how well do you know Lord Portendorfer? I don't mean junior, I mean senior."

"I know next to nothing about him. Why should I?"

"Because..."

Something is wrong. He's thinking about how much he should tell me. Or what he should tell me.

"Lord Portendorfer...is... He shouldn't be taken lightly," said Freyan.

Phoenix shook his head as a smile crept along his lips. "Any man, beast or child who has an army shouldn't be taken lightly, Freyan. This is nothing new to me."

"Lord Portendorfer is--"

"Doesn't he have a first name?"

Freyan slammed his open palm down on the bed, shaking his head. A small sigh escaped him. "Phoenix, Lord Portendorfer is different to Holger. If Holger is the flame from a candle giving light to a room, his father is the sun. The head of the families that make up the Council give up their name and are simply known by their family name."

"Well, that's stupid," said Phoenix.

Freyan stood and walked towards Phoenix. Grabbing him by both shoulders, Freyan once again shook his head. "Before Lord Portendorfer became who he is, he got into an argument with a crime lord who owed him credits. This was before the Council. He was young, angry, and brash, but most of all he was determined. The crime lord's men outnumbered him ten to one. He knew he could never fight them head on, so you know what he did?"

"No," said Phoenix.

"He hid in the camp's latrine for seventy-two hours. With nothing to eat. Nothing to drink. He waited and waited until he found his target, and he shoved his knife... Well, I'm sure you can guess."

"No wonder he gave birth to such a shitty son," said Phoenix with a smile.

Silence filled the room as Freyan simply stared.

"What? Come on, you know that joke was gold."

"Heed my words. If not, at least think them through."

Phoenix patted Freyan on the shoulder before making his way towards the door. He halted with his hand on the handle and looked over his shoulder. "Freyan, it will be all right. Trust me."

"Do you believe what he said?"

"What, Plowstow? Hell no! His story holds up about as well as when I get caught in the bed of a woman I'm not supposed to be with. He's lying through his teeth. I'm just not too sure to what extent. But it doesn't matter, anyway. If he could have sold us out he would have done so already. He knew where we were; all he had to do was pass that message across."

"What if he has something else planned?"

"Highly unlikely," Phoenix said with a snort.

"Why do you keep him around?" Freyan asked.

"Because you can always trust a dishonest dog to do what you expect. Dishonest things. Plowstow is not stupid or evil. He's just greedy and selfish, and I can use that against him. I can use him how I see fit. We have a saying on Earth: better the devil you know."

"It seems like you're the one to be feared," said Freyan.

"I am. But Plowstow doesn't realise that, yet. When he does, it will be too late."

37

Darkness.

Darkness and the smell of fear.

L had learnt the scent of it when she was in Dredar. You didn't recognise it, at first. You didn't accept it. But the longer you stayed around it, the more it seeped into your pores, through your veins, like a toxin. It wrapped itself round you like a tight-fitting mechanic's glove.

She didn't want to accept it was here.

She had grown up since that first night in Dredar. She had told herself, time and time again, that she would not allow herself to become fear's slave. But here she was again. Fighting to breathe. Fighting to think. Trying to keep her heart rate down.

She would be saved. She would be saved.

She had made friends now. Midnight would come to her rescue. Phoenix had promised her that he would not let any harm come to her, no matter what. Phoenix had promised.

He had promised, hadn't he?

"You think you're safe, little girl?" a voice whispered in the darkness.

It made L's spine crawl. She jerked her head left to right but couldn't see anything. The blindfold prevented light from hitting her retinas. L moved her head, trying to detect the location of the voice.

"You think that your friends will come and help you? How wrong you are, my little flower. Friends are friends until a better option comes around. Friends are friends until they have to put themselves in harm's way. There are a few true ones, but how many do you think you have in that little crew of yours? Hmm, I wonder, I wonder. Strange indeed."

L tried to speak but her mouth was dry. She licked her cracked lips and tried again. "Who are you?"

"Me? Some call me the Bell Man–silly name, really. But most call me Rustem."

"What do you want from me?" L asked.

L heard nothing but the gentle jingle of bells. With each passing minute, they grew louder and louder until it felt like they were assaulting her senses.

"Have you ever been raped?" Rustem asked.

The question hung in the air like a lead weight tied around a swimmer's ankle.

"I...err..." L coughed.

"No, no, no, my little flower, you have the wrong idea. I would never do such a thing, but I know others that would. Others housed in this building, in fact..."

"My friends--"

"Are not here. I believe we can both help each other, on this darkest of days. You would like to keep your dignity, and I would like to have this mission of mine go smoothly. You do as I say, and we shall both have what we want. There are a lot of people who want to lay hands on you, my little flower. Holger, for one."

L shuddered at the name.

"There, there. He won't even need to know of your existence, if our deal is kept. You're in safe hands."

L could feel hands stroking her face and backed up but couldn't move any further; something solid at her back prevented her from doing so. Fingertips brushed the sides of her face. They raised goosebumps wherever they touched.

"My friends will come for me. And when they do, Mr Bell Man, you will wish that you were never born," said L.

"That's what I am hoping for."

The half glass of brown liquid in front of Phoenix did nothing to soothe his mood. The glass was dirty and cloudy, like his thoughts. He picked it up, stirred the contents and knocked it back in one. It burnt on the way down. He rubbed his face and let out a sigh. The hair on his chin was now slightly longer than stubble.

He tapped his fingers along the wood of the bar, playing a tune to the thoughts that dominated his mind. The crew couldn't stay much longer. Sooner or later someone would come knocking, and when they did, he needed to be prepared.

What to do? What to do?

Phoenix ordered another brown drink. He waved in a "carry-on" motion as the bartender poured until his glass was filled to the brim. Phoenix ignored the look of disdain the bartender threw his way. He wasn't feeling too great about himself. Shit had gotten out of control, and he didn't know if he could right the ship back to where it needed to be.

He had given Plowstow and Saoirse orders, but that was just to get them thinking about something other than their conflict. He didn't know what he would do with the things he'd sent them to get, but he hoped that some idea would strike him. But still he came up blank.

What to do? What to do?

He slammed his fist down on the bar, earning another look from the bartender. Dammit! Wasn't this what he'd asked for? Didn't he want adventure and crazy space stories? Well, he had got what he asked for, and now he was stumped at the first hurdle. Stumped at the first planet he visited. Huh, some great space adventurer he was turning out to be.

What to do? What to do?

He needed a plan. Plans were never his forte, but he needed to come up with one if he didn't want to see his friends die before his eyes. Saoirse was always level-headed and had an iron sense of calm in battle. But once L was in danger, that calm came crashing down like a house of cards.

Then there was Plowstow. Phoenix knew there was more to him than met the eye; he just couldn't figure out what. Or how Plowstow was tied up with the whole thing.

What to do? What to do?

The opposition had more men, more firepower, more resources, while his own group were trying to grab anything that might come in handy. Phoenix placed his head in his hands and groaned into them.

He was up against three people who wanted him dead. No matter what shit storm he was in, Phoenix had never pissed off so many people all at once. One-maybe two–people had wanted to cause him some serious harm in the past. But he had never had this many so bloodthirsty for his downfall.

Did you really think it was going to be this easy?

Phoenix shook his head, resuming tapping his fingers.

They left shiny marks in the grime as he played a beat that slipped him into a trance.

His brain ran through a hundred different scenarios, but each one always ended in bodies riddled with holes. He couldn't see any way out. He couldn't see the light at the end of the tunnel.

They were doomed.

"Shit!

38

A knock on the door made Holger lift his head from the maps he was reading. He ran a hand through his hair and let out an irritated sigh. The table in front of him was covered in star maps, reports and any findings his spies had managed to acquire. Holographic images of different planets vied for space on the walls around him.

The answer was bound to be here somewhere.

Another knock at the door resounded, this one more forceful than the first.

Holger slammed his balled-up fist on the desk and glared at the door. "What?"

"My lord...there is an important call for you," said a voice through the door.

"Take a message! I'm in the middle of something."

"He says it can't wait. He says that because you ain't answering your holocom he was forced to contact the ship itself."

"Who says?" said Holger.

"He says that you wouldn't want his name being known among your crew. That saying his name is like uttering a curse of old; once it is said, the action can't be undone. That once it is known, death will befall all who were not meant to hear it," said the voice through the door.

"I will deal with this issue. You can go back to your post."

Holger slammed his fist down on the desk in front of him once again, scattering papers everywhere. He shook his head and looked around the room. He walked through a door into a different room. The walls of this room were bare, with nothing but cushions and chairs decorating the living space.

Holger punched a code into his holocom and allowed the call to come through. The projection of Rustem's face beamed at him in glee.

"Now, why would you block my calls, when this is such an important job? One of the few rules that I have is that I am able to keep in touch with my client at all times. Jobs like mine are as special as a dying star. Things change, things evolve," said Rustem.

"I am busy. Make it short."

"Surely you are not too busy to hear the good news that I have; news like this can't simply be--"

"Rustem!" Holger barked.

"Fine. Fine. I was just updating you on the fact that I shall have Phoenix in my possession any day now. I have plans--"

"Wait. This is not a call telling me that the task that I have assigned you is complete? I am confused. How is this good news?"

"I thought you would like to know how the job is coming along," said Rustem.

"Then you thought wrong, didn't you?" Holger's eyes flicked to a flashing light on his holocom. He sucked his teeth in irritation. "The next call I want from you is one to inform me that the job is done. Until then, I do not want to be interrupted again. Now, there is a call coming through that I must take. Do not disappoint me, Rustem."

The last image Holger got was of Rustem's lips pulled back in a fine line. A small vein pulsed along his temple. *Good.* Holger hoped that the mercenary was angry at being dismissed so quickly. The sooner he learnt his place, the better.

Holger took a seat in one of the chairs that littered the room. Back straight, stomach pulled in, he brushed down the sleeves of his jacket before allowing the call to come through.

Ajax's face appeared before him. The scar along his jaw shone as his jaw clenched. His hands were balled in front of him, one resting in the other. They were huge. Meant for choking necks and cracking skulls.

"Ajax. To what do I owe this honour? I can't believe you would take time out of your *training* to talk to someone like me. Has father still got you running around doing little errands for him? Thought you would be sick of having a boot on your neck for so long. But, alas, if that's all you have ever known..."

"Are you out of your mind, boy?"

"Boy?" said Holger.

"I asked you a question."

"Not the last time that I checked, no, Ajax. I am quite sound in mind. I have never felt better. Now, can you tell me what this call is all about?"

"You appear to be digging into affairs that do not concern you. I am told that you are looking for another planet so you can try and acquire their resources--"

"Have you, now! I didn't think what I did would reach

such lofty ears as yours, Ajax. What I do with my time is my own business, no one--"

"In that you are mistaken, boy. What you do affects the whole family. Your actions ripple far and wide. You think you can act as you want? Do as you please? You are wrong. Wrong and arrogant. I have told you that no moves can be made in trying to find more resources or invading another planet; the Council will not have it. We must tread lightly."

"The Council would never know," said Holger.

"If I found out, the Council already knows, or is at least looking into it. Cease all operations you have going in this endeavour. Clean your tracks as best you can. You are fortunate that I found this out before it reached your father's ears. His actions would not have been as kind," said Ajax.

"But--"

"No buts, Holger! Just get it done. Don't make me clean up another of your messes." With that, the image of Ajax disappeared.

Holger sat slumped in his chair, as if the strings holding him up had been cut. His cheeks were red, his mouth dry, his hand was wet. Holger allowed a snarl to escape his lips.

Who does he think he is? Telling me what to do. Instructing me? They will see! They will all see my greatness!

Then their fear will come and I will bathe in it.

39

Phoenix stood with his hands clenched tightly behind his back. Everyone had gathered in the little room the crew had claimed as theirs. It stank of too many bodies, but beggars couldn't be choosers; it would have to do for the time being. Faces looked up at Phoenix in apprehension. Saoirse's lips were tight and fire filled her eyes. Freyan had a pleasant smile and a relaxed demeanour. Lastly Plowstow shifted his gaze back and forth like a caged rat, looking for a way out. Thinking that maybe this was a trap. That maybe this was where it all ended.

Phoenix lifted his head and inhaled deeply. It didn't smell pretty, but pretty wasn't what he needed right now.

"I'm not going to lie to you and tell you that this will be easy. If you think it will be, erase that thought from your mind. I'm not going to tell you that if we fail then it doesn't matter. It does. It fucking does. It matters what happens out there, because they have one of our friends. But more importantly, they are threatening our friend's family. Our crewmate! We must do whatever we can to ensure that we do not fail--"

"But the odds, Phoenix," said Plowstow.

"Fuck the odds! None of us got where we are by listening to the odds. By allowing the odds to govern what we do. We got here because we spat in the odds' face and told him we ain't listening to his shit!"

Phoenix could feel the blood rushing to his face. He paced back and forth, as the slowly building rage sharpened his mind. It had been cloudy, uncertain, hesitant, but now, it carved a path to where it knew he needed to be.

"But we're up against Rustem and Duke!" said Plowstow.

"Oh, don't forget Holger, as well," said Freyan cheerfully.

"So? You going to let some short angry gangster push you around?"

"I just--"

"Think of it this way, Plowstow: whatever you find that is Duke's, after this is over, you get to keep. Any loot whatsoever," Phoenix said with a smile.

The glint in Plowstow's eyes could outshine the brightest star on a cloudless night. He nodded his head up and down and licked his lips. Phoenix was surprised he didn't start rubbing his hands in glee.

"You can keep as much of it as you can carry, my friend. You can take it all! Jewels, weapons, credits. Whatever you find, you may have."

"This plan of yours–is it sufficient to complete the task at hand?" asked Saoirse.

"I won't lie to you, Saoirse, I've had better ideas. But this is the best I can think of. We'll run over it till it makes you happy. Any suggestions you have are more than welcome. We won't move till everyone is happy," said Phoenix.

She gave him a small nod but didn't say anything else.

"I am sick of people taking what's ours! It's time to start taking it back!"

40

Duke sat behind his desk, eyes narrowed, as he looked across to Rustem. Rustem leaned back in his chair, eyes half closed, with his feet on Duke's desk and his hands laced behind his head.

Duke bit the inside of his cheek to stop his rage from spilling out. Rustem and his men had made themselves at home in Duke's warehouse. Duke wanted to club each and every one of their brains out but he needed Rustem...for the moment.

"So... What's so important that you saw it necessary to interrupt me in the middle of my work?" Duke asked.

"Can a new friend not greet another without there being something they need from each other? Why can't we enjoy each other's company? Why can't we just be, without there being this uneasy feeling?" said Rustem.

"Because you're a murderous worm that will kill anything just to benefit you," said Duke.

"How dare you insult my good name? I will have you know that I only kill for business. I am an entrepreneur, and murder is the business I deal in. I have stopped civil wars that would have claimed millions of lives. I liberated billions, by killing dictators that enslaved and tortured their people. I have killed scientists that were creating weapons of mass destruction. But I will admit that in between that and this, I have killed children, women and innocent souls. My slate may not be clean, but it sparkles compared to yours."

"I do not lie to myself so I can sleep at night," said Duke. "I am what I am. I accepted that role a long time ago. I was created from the sand and will return there when the time comes. Till then, I will take whatever I can, as others have taken from me!"

"How petty. Like a child only wanting what's in front of his face, not having the foresight to see the bigger picture. It's a shame you shall die with those eyes of yours never fully opened," said Rustem.

"Will you be the one to complete that task?" Duke asked, grabbing the edge of the desk, his hands turning white.

"Me?" Rustem questioned, touching his chest. "Oh, no. Not I. I shall allow that honour to be had by someone else. Someone more deserving than I. Why would I wish to take your life when you have hardly offended me at all?"

"Hardly?"

"No, your fate does not lie in my hands. I can guarantee you that," Rustem said, swapping the placement of his feet on the desk, and in doing so letting large amounts of dirt drop from his boots.

"But what if yours lies in mine?" Duke smiled.

Rustem threw his head back and a laugh escaped his lips. "Many have tried to claim what is not theirs. Many have tried to add my name to their accomplishments. But, as you can see, I am still standing. I have been told that you own a few gambling houses. Maybe you would like to try your luck." Rustem took out a small knife and whirled it around his fingers till the blade became a blur.

Duke watched the blade silently, left hand drumming along the desk, right hand playing the same tune on the handle of his pistol. *I wonder who is faster... Argh! Another time maybe.*

"If you have nothing of importance to discuss, then..." Duke pointed towards the door.

"How the pleasantries of small talk have been lost. Very well, I will get to the meat of the conversation. I have had word that Phoenix wants to meet, to broker some sort of deal. I will give you the location, as we are partners in this endeavour."

"Partners, are we, now?" said Duke.

"Yes, partners. To build some trust between us, I will allow L to be contained in this building alongside her brother. I think--"

"Now, why would you do that? What's stopping me from killing you once she is in this building?"

"Because you need my men. For this to go smoothly, you will need all the bodies you can get. Since I have made that number a bit...smaller, since my arrival, you can class it as a gift," said Rustem.

"Well, I'm all sorts of lucky today, ain't I?"

"One condition: I stay here. *You* meet Phoenix."

Duke's eyes narrowed as he leaned back in his chair.

There was a game being played here, but he couldn't see where it ended. Rustem wanted Phoenix, so why not go get the Earth man himself? Why wait here? If Duke got to Phoenix first, he could use the Earth man as bargaining power over Rustem.

Hell. Why stop there? It would be easier to cut out the middle-man completely and sell to Rustem's client. He would just have to find out who that was, first. But once he did, he could ask whatever price he wanted. The only thing that stood in his way was Rustem.

Maybe the Bell Man did come bearing gifts.

"If you insist," Duke said with a smile.

Rustem got to his feet and gave Duke a small nod. He turned on his heels and gestured for one of his men to follow him.

"Rustem. Is he one of yours?" Duke asked, pointing to the man.

"Yes."

"Good." Duke drew his pistol and fired a shot between the man's eyes. Smoke wafted from the hole the plasma bolt left, and the smell of burnt flesh crept into the room. The body collapsed in a heap on the floor.

"As you're on your way out, see to that, will you, Rustem?"

"He--"

"I always have enough men. Just remember that," said Duke.

41

The setting sun looked like a fireball being swallowed by the sands, its dying light giving the sand before Phoenix's feet a golden tint. Phoenix squatted low and scooped up a handful, allowing the sand to run between his fingers.

Golden. Beautiful. Warm.

Phoenix blew the last remains from his hand and watched them dance on the breeze. It wouldn't take long for the breeze to feel like needles against the skin, as the rapidly changing temperature went from one extreme to the other.

But he was hoping to be back in the city by then.

The temperature wouldn't play much of a factor anyway, as he was covered from head to toe in combat gear. The jet-black material felt like Kevlar and fitted him like a second skin. It regulated his temperature and protected him against plasma bolts. Bolt guns and anything larger would still do damage.

He tore his gaze from the horizon and looked behind him. Saoirse and Plowstow each straddled a hover bike, also kitted out in combat gear. The rusty brown bikes blended into their surroundings, and the slight pulse they emitted from their undercarriages shifted the sand around them.

Both carried a wide array of weaponry. It appeared Saoirse had stolen an armoury. Phoenix had wanted to ask if she had acquired them in an honourable way, but his nerve gave out on him.

Saoirse had gone back to being quiet and still. Phoenix wanted to reach out and lend an ear, but he knew that her pride wouldn't allow her to open up. She dealt with things in her own way–through violence mostly.

Phoenix looked up to see the faint outlines of stars starting to emerge in the sky. He breathed through his nose and allowed the air to calm him down.

He hoped this worked.

Yet another simple plan. Yet another risk that might end his life.

"Phoenix, you sure this will work? I mean, I'm too young to die out here...among the worm shit...and...and...sand."

"Plowstow, honestly, hope for the best, expect the worst. That's the only guarantee I can give you."

"That ain't much of a guarantee."

"Think of the loot, Plowstow. Think of the loot," said Phoenix.

"I'm thinking. I'm thinking--"

"Don't hurt yourself," said Saoirse.

"And I'm thinking that maybe loot isn't all worth it. Maybe a nice quiet life would do me just fine, you know? Find a home, find a female–maybe two–because the nights get cold--"

A snort from Saoirse drew a quick sideways glance from Plowstow.

"Raise a family. Maybe buy some land. You know, just

live all peaceful-like. Maybe grow some crops. Shit! I don't know, Phoenix, just do something less risky than this shit."

Phoenix let out a small laugh and shook his head. "Really, Plowstow, you think that sort of life is for you? Getting moaned at all the time. Not being able to come and go as you please. Never seeing the unknown worlds that could house all sorts of rare and valuable treasure. Growing older and poorer, each and every day, because your offspring are taking every credit you have. Does that sound like fun to you?"

Silence.

Phoenix looked over his shoulder and saw Plowstow's eyes widen with fear.

"By the pit demon of Rag, no!" Plowstow slapped himself in the face before saying. "If you ever hear me utter such shit again, beat me silly."

"I'll be glad to," said Saoirse.

He's scared. Good.

That should keep Plowstow alive and sharp. If Phoenix just kept the Orcian's mind on what he could make out of this deal, then he would have one less problem to worry about. This plan needed everyone on board or it just wouldn't work.

Phoenix sat on his hover bike and noticed dust in the distance. Even in the fading light, he could see it trailing like signal smoke up in the air.

"Right, ladies and gentlemen. It's showtime!"

42

Phoenix watched the convoy approach like a desert viper. They weren't coming in fast; they were taking their time. Showing Phoenix that his time wasn't worth their haste. That although he had summoned them there, they were still in charge.

How little they knew.

"Check your weapons. I don't think this will be a friendly discussion," said Phoenix.

He leaned on his bike and squinted into the distance to get a better look at what was coming. Four hover pickup trucks, ten hover bikes. *Well, looks like they brought their full force out to play.* That was good. It would give Freyan time to work.

"It appears they don't want to take any chances. It is wise of them," said Saoirse.

"I was hoping that I made that little fucker so mad that he'd come rushing out here all by himself. Well, there's still time, I guess," said Phoenix.

"It appears Rustem is not with them," said Saoirse.

"I figured as much. They wouldn't risk leaving L and Kai alone, but I have faith in Freyan."

The vehicles approaching the trio had bits of metal bolted and welded to them for sharp edges to stick out. Barbed wire encircled a few like skirts. Phoenix could see mounted cannons poking out of the back of the trucks. Bodies hung out of both vehicles, banging against the sides with their weapons. Their war cries carried on the breeze.

"They appear to be excited," said Saoirse.

"That will soon change," Phoenix replied.

"They appear unafraid."

"That will also change."

Phoenix's heart raced, and he took a breath to steady it. He ran his tongue over his dry lips and wiped his damp hands on his jacket.

Now wasn't the time for second guesses. Now wasn't the time for doubts.

As the convoy came into full view, it began to circle the crew. Round and round it went, kicking sand up into the air so it was impossible to see clearly. Phoenix covered his mouth as the dust tried to make its way into his system.

Shouts and curses could be heard just beyond the wall of sand. Phoenix dodged as something was thrown his way. His vision was limited. His hearing was feeding him too much stimulus.

Scare tactics.

Phoenix's shoulders began to shake as laughter began to erupt from the depths of his soul. These fools had underestimated him. They had underestimated his crew. *How little they knew.*

The convoy slowed and came to a stop in front of them. As the dust settled, and the vehicles stopped in their various spots,

Phoenix swept his gaze over them. What he saw didn't impress him. The mean mugging, the gun toting, the threatening behaviour, spoke volumes about who he was dealing with.

They might have been accustomed to violence, but they were clueless in the art of terror. Phoenix tried to wipe the smug look from his face but it wouldn't go away.

Duke stepped out of one of the hover pickup trucks and strutted over as if he had a rod firmly shoved up his ass.

Rookie move. Stay with your vehicle at all times. You may need to escape or pursue your enemy. He must think very little of us indeed.

Duke came to a stop and placed his hands on his hips. He took in the three bikes and their riders. His gaze flitted from one masked face to the next. "So...which of you is Phoenix? Phoenix Jones? I didn't catch your name before you ran out of my building like a scared little child."

"All depends who is asking, really. The answer is different for an angry husband, a jealous ex or an anyone in-between."

"Don't play games with me! I know--" Duke let out a heavy sigh and pinched the bridge of his nose. "I know who you are, Phoenix, so please do not play games with me. It will not end well for you."

"Big threats made by a little Dukey," Phoenix said with a smile.

Plowstow burst out laughing, doing nothing to improve the mood.

"You really think you're all that, don't ya?" Duke said. "Smooth-talking, big-walking, chest-puffing, king of all he surveys. I have seen a hundred like you. There will be a hundred more to come, and do you know where they will all end up? Right here." Duke said, kicking sand towards Phoenix.

"You've never seen anything like me."

"Oh, is that so?"

"If you had, you wouldn't be alive, right now. You should be happy that none were like me, because you got to live out your days–until now."

"Is that so?" Duke said, smirking over his shoulder at his laughing men.

"I'm afraid it is."

Duke smiled at Phoenix. "You hear that, boys?" he called over his shoulder. "I should be happy to be alive. Me! Me! Who has taken what he saw fit?"

"You!" rang the cries from his men.

"Who pulled his way out from the gutter to the throne?"

"You!" yelled the voices at Duke's back.

"Who gave you somewhere to live? Something to do? Made you into something that you could be proud of?"

"You! You! You! You!"

Duke spread his arms wide and beamed in Phoenix's direction.

"They matter little, when you face me. But this you will learn in time. Now, where are my crewmates?" said Phoenix.

"*Crewmate,* fucker."

"Young Kai will be coming with us, along with L. Now, I will not repeat myself. Where. Are. My. *Crewmates?*"

Duke lifted his hands in the air and gave Phoenix a puzzled stare. He shook his head and began to laugh; holding his sides he continued on and on.

Expressionless, Phoenix waited for him to finish.

"I get it, now. You're out of your fucking mind. Completely and utterly. Do you not see how the odds are stacked against you? Do you not see that you're outnumbered more than three to one? What were you expecting when you called me out here? You, Phoenix Jones, have nothing to offer. Nothing to bargain with. I am not the only one that wants your head.

"Yet you send a message to meet me in the middle of the desert. Not in a crowded place. Not somewhere that you would have the advantage. No, in the fucking desert. Any sane person would run and get off-world, lost among the stars. Any smart person would never meet me like this. But you–you–I see are a special case. Part stupid, part crazy. Ahh, this was fun. I will miss you when you're gone," said Duke.

"Are you done?" Phoenix asked.

Duke gave him a small nod.

"I will ask one more time. Do you have my people?"

"No, dum-dum. I do not."

"Well, I guess you die." As the words left Phoenix's mouth, an explosion lifted the sand into the air like a tsunami.

43

L didn't know how long she had been kept in the room. It could have been mere hours or it could have been days. Whenever she demanded something to eat or drink she was taken to a different room and fed before being placed back in the room where darkness ruled. The same thing happened if she needed the toilet.

On one of her trips out of the dark room, thoughts of escape surfaced. But her ideas were quickly dashed against the rocks and sank like a ship, because more than one guard always escorted her anywhere she went.

She got up and stretched her back until it popped. At least they had taken off her restraints, so she could wander around in the dark as she pleased. It had taken more than a few falls and bruised shins for her to get a feel for the layout of the room.

"If this is what being blind is like, then you can keep it," L muttered to herself.

How was she ever going to get out of there? There were no windows or vents to escape through, and when the door locked it sealed into the wall completely. She ran her hands back and forth along the wall, but she couldn't find any way to prise it open. She had spoken a good game to Rustem but doubts were beginning to creep along the edges of her subconscious.

What if Midnight never found her? What if Phoenix decided she wasn't worth the trouble? They had only just met, after all; there were no real bonds of friendship between them. Who even was she to him? Some ship's engineer that he could replace at the click of his fingers.

L let out a sigh and ran her hands through her hair.

The click of the door brought her attention to the present. The harshness of the light that spilled out of the entrance assaulted her senses, forcing her to turn away. She heard someone yell as they fell forward into the room and the door was locked again with a slam and a hiss.

L brought her head back round to where she last saw the door; light spots still danced in front of her face.

"H-he-hello?" said a voice through the darkness.

"Kai?"

"L?"

"Well, if this isn't a fine how-do-you-do? They lock me up in complete darkness, then they throw you in here to torment me. What did I ever do to deserve this? I was just a simple engineer, attracted to the big city lights, who brought her halfwit brother along.

"If only I'd known what trouble you would cause me, Kai. If I only I'd known what trouble you would fill my life with, I would have left you back in that cave we called a village. Do you remember what it was like there?"

"I remember, L," said Kai.

"Do you? Do you! Do you remember the cold winds so strong that we lost more than one family member to sickness? The roar of hungry stomachs till they no longer made a sound?"

"I remember."

"The constant fear of attacks from worms? The raids from bandits so hungry they looked like skeletons wearing rags?"

"I remember."

"The constant fear, terror, heartache, loneliness--"

"I remember! All right, L! I remember all of it. I was there too, you know, or have you forgotten? You may think you had it just as hard as I, but I had it longer. I was alive through it longer, I had to endure it longer. I know how it was...I know. I thought the universe was empty. Thought it was a heartless, soulless place. I lost my faith in everything. I almost gave up believing in the faith of Soul. I..."

L heard the faintest of footsteps come forward then stop.

"I...I had given up faith, that day you found me in the desert. I lied and said I was following you, but in fact it was just by chance, fate, destiny, that we met. Do you know what I was doing there?" said Kai.

L shook her head but realised that Kai couldn't see her. "No."

"I was going there to die."

L wanted to gasp but she couldn't make a sound. Instead her mouth hung open, and she stared at the dark where she believed Kai must stand before her.

"I was just going to walk the land till I died of thirst, got eaten by a worm or attacked by bandits. Whichever way death came first, I would embrace it. I had completely lost hope in everything," said Kai.

L placed a hand to her mouth. Again, she tried to speak but nothing came out. Her heart faltered then missed a beat.

Swallowing the lump in her throat, she said, "But why? You always seemed the heart and soul of the family."

Kai let out a bitter laugh. "Do you know how hard that was? Do you know how difficult it got, day by day, night by night, preaching the words of Soul but seeing death in front of your eyes? Friends, lovers, family members. In the name of Soul, it was rough. It was rough having that weight on my shoulders.

"So I walked and walked, and just by chance, just by fate, I met you. I knew it wasn't an accident. I knew I had to follow you."

"Why?"

"VRG. Don't laugh, I think it was. I know I can't hit the side of a hundred-foot worm when I play the game, but I have a skill where I can programme it and bring joy to people's lives. Give them a few hours away from the pain of their lives. To me that is magical," said Kai.

"Really, Kai?"

"What are the words of the faith of Soul, L? Love. Laugh. Dance. Hallucinate. Do I not create all four of those things when people play my VRG games?"

"We both know hallucinate normally means to take a shitload of drugs," L said with a laugh.

"So what, baby sis? Can't a brother read between the lines?" Kai said with a chuckle.

"But you were always good with computer programmes. You were always gifted," said L.

"I just found better uses for that gift. That's all."

Silence and darkness stood between the two siblings; neither knew what to say next. L remembered when nobody could keep them apart. She remembered when they had both laughed. When they both got into trouble for hiking into the desert without a backward glance. How things had changed. Well, not so much, she thought. They were still getting into trouble. Each still being punished for the things the other had done.

"L, I never meant for any of this to happen. Just...one thing led to another. I'm sorry. I love you. And I will do whatever I can to protect you."

"Kai...I know, I know."

44

Sand erupted into the air as explosion after explosion went off all around them. A column of flame punched one hover pickup thirty feet in the air. Over and over it spun as bodies were thrown from its interior like shrapnel from a bomb. The burning wreckage landed nose first on top of another pickup, crushing those inside it.

Two bikes disintegrated into a million pieces as an explosion ripped them apart. Shards of the bikes tore into flesh without mercy, and screams howled into the night sky like wolves on a hunt.

The explosions seemed to go on and on, spewing fiery vomit into the desert air. Those who were not prepared for the onslaught cowered and dived for cover.

Phoenix stood motionless, watching the chaos unfold. Sand rained down from the heavens and covered all. Black smoke stung the eyes. The smell of burnt flesh invaded the nostrils.

Phoenix was stunned by the carnage they had caused. Twisted metal decorated the desert like modern art. Bodies lay mangled and half-buried. He felt frozen in time, looking at the wreckage around him. He didn't feel part of it. There was so much chaos but time itself felt slowed down.

He saw eyes widen in panic. He saw mouths agape, frozen in fear. Others held severed limbs, desperately trying to re-attach them.

Through all of it, Phoenix stood motionless, detached, until it felt like an ice-cold bucket of water poured itself over his head. It started from the base of his neck and worked its way down.

That felt...weird.

Phoenix felt his reality come back with a pop, like a movie playing at normal speed after moving frame by frame.

"Saoirse, how much explosives did you use?" Phoenix asked.

"Just the right amount," the midnight-blue demon smirked.

Flames scorched the sand. Blood poured from wounds. Screams bellowed from mouths. But the initial shock of the attack was starting to wear off, and gang members started to come to their senses. They still appeared to have some fight left in them. Phoenix would have to change that.

"Light them up!" Phoenix yelled.

Three bolt rifles fired without mercy, punching the desert air like heavyweight boxers. Phoenix aimed and fired, taking out anything that crossed his path.

A hover biker took a bolt that tore his head clean off. Phoenix shot a bike from underneath another and watched in satisfaction as it spun out of control and collided with another making its way towards them.

"Do not let them escape! I don't care what Rustem says–kill them all," said Duke, ducking and diving for cover.

Phoenix fired off shot after shot, trying to hit the gang leader, but he was always a second or two too late. "Slippery bastard."

Duke's remaining men had begun to collect themselves. The shots fired at Phoenix's crew were becoming more and more precise. Terror and fear no longer made for unsteady hands; they were getting over Phoenix's shock and awe attack. He had hoped to pick off a few more before they collected themselves. As things stood, the numbers were too high for him to take them all out in an open gunfight.

Phoenix ducked as something pinged off his handlebars. "Saoirse, do you have anymore explosives up those beautiful sleeves of yours?"

"Beautiful?" Even in the midst of battle, where life and death hung by a thread, the look Saoirse gave Phoenix told him there was more to fear than weapon fire if he spoke to her like that again.

"What, can't I give you a simple compliment?"

The stare continued.

"Are we going to do this right now? Really?" said Phoenix.

"No, I do not have any other explosives up my *sleeves*. Or anywhere else, for that matter. They have been all spent."

"Shit. Plowstow, you--" Two more pings hit the side of Phoenix's bike. He ducked as a plasma bolt passed inches from his head. "You got anything?"

"Nah, all out."

Phoenix turned towards his foes and saw that they were beginning to get organised. They were spread out in an arc, pushing their way towards the crew. The latter needed to make a move towards the city and fight them there. Out here they were outnumbered and outgunned, sitting ducks waiting for slaughter.

"Phoenix Jones! You believe you could have won, but out here...the desert winds change victory into defeat quicker than you can blink. It's a shame that this is where you will die. So far from home," said Duke.

"Big words, little Dukey. Why don't you show yourself instead of cowering behind your men?"

There was a moment's ceasefire as both parties looked at each other, searching for any signs of weakness. Neither party wanted to make the first move.

"I will gladly--"

A scream from one of Duke's men cut his words short. Panic ran through their ranks as they looked for another unseen enemy. Darkness had descended around the battleground like death's cloak.

One minute it was light, then it wasn't. Confusion reigned and vehicle lights were switched on so they could scan the area around them. Another scream echoed in the darkness.

"What's going on?" yelled Duke.

Phoenix looked to Saoirse and Plowstow, who both gave him blank stares. Who had come to help them in their hour of need? Freyan was in the city, and Phoenix knew of no one else that would risk their life to help them.

Phoenix brought his weapon up to finish off what he had started when he saw something that stilled his heart. There was movement in the sand.

45

The air was tense as sand shifted and moved in the night. What Phoenix thought he saw had vanished before he had time to flash his light on it.

All had gone silent again.

Everyone seemed to hold their breath. Waiting. Wondering. Nobody moved a muscle; they all moved as one, illuminating and scanning the area around them. They had fought as bitter enemies but a few moments ago, but when things that lurked in the darkness appeared before them, enemies quickly turned into allies.

"You think these tricks will work on me?" Duke asked. "I have seen better--"

"Shut up, you fool! Something else is at play here," said Saoirse.

"Who is this female that dares to speak to me? I will--"

Another scream cut Duke off, but this time light bathed the offender, illuminating his face for the world to see. It wasn't a pretty picture to behold. Eyes so wide that it seemed they would pop out at any moment stared out into a void that none could see. His was a face that stared into death's hollow eyes and knew his time was up. He sank to his chest in the desert sand, his hands clawing for purchase. Try as he might, he couldn't get a firm enough grip and he sank deeper and deeper into the sand.

He fought and fought, but it was of no use. He disappeared in the sand and all that remained were the grooves clawed into the sand by his fingertips.

The whole thing had happened without anyone uttering a word. Not the person who had been attacked. Not his friends, who stood and watched helplessly. It had played out like a silent movie, as if adding sound to the scene they witnessed was a detail too much.

"We are in a worm nest! Get out before it's too late," cried a voice.

Phoenix didn't need to hear the warning twice. He signaled Saoirse and Plowstow, and they took off on their bikes. Phoenix fired as many shots as he could at Duke's scattered troops. A male with a Mohawk two feet tall ran alongside Phoenix's bike, trying to get on. He gripped the side of the bike and tried to hold on. Phoenix almost felt sorry for the man as he stared into a face that showed nothing but fear. Then he remembered L.

Phoenix took out his pistol and fired point-blank between the gang member's eyes. The man's hands still refused to let go, clutching at the side of the bike in a death grip. Phoenix kicked the body clear and sent it tumbling into the sand. He looked back to see the body disappear beneath the sand.

"That went better than expected! All we need to do now is get to the city before them and pick them off one--"

Phoenix was cut off and veered left as an explosion kicked up sand that splattered against the side of his face.

The smoking hole the explosion left gave Phoenix all the incentive he needed to twist the throttle and go. Over his shoulder he could see lights in the distance–they were heading their way. Another bright flash from one of the pickup cannons and more sand exploded far too close for Phoenix's liking.

"Fan out! It will make us harder targets to hit. Head for the junkyard behind Duke's warehouse," said Phoenix.

"What do we do if we get lost? I don't wanna die out here with those things," said Plowstow.

"Then don't get lost," said Phoenix.

Phoenix caught Saoirse's eye, but neither said anything. She simply smiled and nodded her head before taking off ahead of him. He turned in his seat and saw Duke's men closing in. They were gaining ground faster than he'd expected.

Hundred-foot worms chewing at your ass–that tends to give you all the motivation you need to move quickly.

Three explosions just ahead of them forced Phoenix to duck and weave through smoke and flames. Sand pelleted his back as it descended again. A bike pulled up alongside him, and the owner tried to steady his aim and fire his pistol. Phoenix slammed his bike into the attacker's, lifting his leg out of the way at the last minute. As the two bikes collided, the attacker's leg was trapped between them. Even over the roar of the engines and the sound of bombs, Phoenix still heard the crunch as bone shattered into a hundred bits.

The attacker's scream sent a chill down Phoenix's spine.

Phoenix pulled away and saw the gang member reach for his leg with a tentative hand. He should have been paying attention to where he was going, but the pain from his leg seemed to be all he could focus on. He failed to see a boulder jutting out from under the sand. His bike slammed into the rock, flipping twice before it came crashing down on top of the rider's body.

Phoenix didn't give it a second look.

Another explosion; another face full of sand. Phoenix stared straight ahead at the city lights, blinking and twinkling enticingly, waving him onwards, inviting him to safety. All he had to do was make it there alive.

"Mr Jones!" a voice called in the darkness.

Phoenix snapped his head around, looking for the owner. Duke's grinning face met him from the hovering pickup truck next to him. Phoenix gave him a friendly wave before opening fire. None of the shots hit their target, but they did cause the driver to swerve.

Movement in the sand to his left stole his attention. A long body, hidden under the sand, snaked alongside the bike. It wasn't as big as the first one he had seen when he arrived on the planet, but it was indeed big enough to cause him concern. Phoenix looked on in horror as a black body at least thirty feet in length, covered with diamond-shaped scales, rose from the sand. Its armour-plated skin was beautiful to behold. Phoenix looked at the long tubular body and eyeless head in wonder. The barbels along either side of the worm's head searched the air like a sniffer dog's nose.

Phoenix began to pull away from the creature but it sensed him. Its barbels pointed in Phoenix's direction and the creature's round head swung his way. It dived under the sand and began to follow him. The thing was fast–too fast for something of its size.

A thought lurked in the back of Phoenix's mind; one that he tried to keep at bay. The size of these worms meant most were not fully grown. If that was the case, then one question remained that they should all be concerned about. Where were the parents?

"Mr Jones!"

Phoenix turned at the sound of his name and saw something that stopped his heart. A bolt pistol pointed in his direction. Time slowed as Phoenix looked at the weapon. Seeing the shooter's body hanging out of the truck, arm steady, ready to take aim, Phoenix knew two things: that no matter how bad a shot the shooter was, he couldn't miss, and Phoenix wouldn't be able to move out of the way in time, no matter what he did.

"Goodbye!"

46

Phoenix knew with certainty that he was dead meat.

There were so many things he had yet to see. So many places he had yet to go. How could his journey end on the first planet his feet touched? It didn't seem fair, somehow. It didn't seem right.

What's ever right, asshole? Be glad you got to see what you did. Be glad you got to experience what you did. Be glad you got to meet the people and cultures you did. Nothing is guaranteed, in this life or the next.

Phoenix accepted his fate, and a smile broke across his lips like the first rays of the sun at dawn.

A worm erupted from the sand without warning. Its head reared up in between Phoenix's bike and the truck, and the worm latched onto its prey. The shooter screamed as a scaly black head clamped onto his body. Teeth dripping with black ooze sank into flesh. The shooter held onto the rails of the truck with both hands, pistol all but forgotten.

Phoenix could hear bones snap, one by one, as the worm increased its pressure.

"Duke! Help me! For the love of Soul, help me!"

But there was no help to be found. The worm shook its head once, twice, and the shooter's grip gave out and he was pulled off the truck. His body disappeared into the sand amidst screams of pain.

Phoenix stared behind him, stunned. He made eye contact with Duke, who gave a simple shrug before diving for the dropped pistol.

Phoenix knew he had to act fast. Sweeping his bike towards the pickup, he waited till the last moment and dived into the back of the truck, landing on Duke. The two went down in a heap. Phoenix heard the pistol clatter to the floor. Duke was unarmed–or so Phoenix thought until a blade swept across his face.

Phoenix leapt back out of reach. He got to his feet as Duke began to do the same. Duke stood with his feet apart and tossed his knife from hand to hand. Phoenix patted himself down, looking for a weapon. Coming up short, a frown crept across his features.

Shit. I must have dropped my pistol.

"Lost something?" Duke said with a laugh.

"No. I was just making sure that I had nothing on me. I want this to be a fair fight," said Phoenix.

"You little--"

"Hah! Look who's talking," Phoenix laughed.

"I have never met a creature more irritating than you. More arrogant than you. It shall be my pleasure to put an end to your life."

"Come on then, Dukey! Show me that you can at least swing your fist past my balls!"

Duke roared as he came towards Phoenix, his face twisted in a snarl. Phoenix could feel his intent radiating off him–pure anger. He wanted nothing more than to inflict as much pain on Phoenix as he could.

There wasn't much room to move, but Phoenix leaned out of the way of Duke's first strike. He would have to disarm Duke fast. The lack of room only worked in Duke's favour, and he hacked and swung his way towards Phoenix.

Duke only had to be lucky once–a cut artery here, a slashed tendon there. It would take no time at all for Phoenix to bleed out. If the cut was bad enough, all Duke had to do was wait Phoenix out.

"Come on! Is that all you have? Is that all you're worth?" Phoenix taunted.

Duke's snarl deepened as he slashed left to right–wild, angry, uncoordinated.

Phoenix took a chance and stepped forward, but Duke slashed him across the chest. Phoenix took in a sharp breath. He expected pain but none came. Bringing his hand to his chest, he noticed that the combat gear he was wearing had stopped the cut. A faint line ran across the material.

"It looks like your little suit saved you. But how many cuts do you think it can stop? Won't it be fun trying to find out?" said Duke.

"Duke, tell me something, will you? How did a short, ugly little shit like yourself ever get into power? I mean, at the first sign of you approaching, anyone with half a brain would just stomp you out like the insect you are," said Phoenix.

"People respect power, no matter the size–"

The punch Phoenix delivered snapped Duke's head back and flattened his nose against his face. Phoenix delivered a kick to his stomach before he had to lean back as Duke slashed the blade towards him.

"Yeah, I wasn't really interested in a reply, if I'm honest. But I will give you one word of advice: if you believe power is the only thing that counts in this life, you're wrong.

Power-hungry fools, such as yourself, think gaining more power will chase away the demons that haunt you. You think power is only about fear, which is short-sighted. Fear is like a twisted tree that strangles its own roots to survive."

Duke let out a yawn as he launched himself at Phoenix again. "Nothing but pretty words. Pretty words won't save you here!"

The attack was sloppy. Anger had clouded Duke's vision. Phoenix ducked the blade, as it sailed close to his face, and hit Duke square in the chest with his shoulder. Phoenix heard the breath escape Duke's lungs. He didn't give the gang leader a chance to recover, and lifted his head straight up into Duke's chin. The blow hurt; it dazed Phoenix slightly, but he knew Duke would come off worse.

Phoenix wrapped his arms around Duke and rushed him to the edge of the truck. He squeezed with all his might, shaking Duke till he dropped his knife.

The moment of victory was short-lived, as Duke's knee sunk itself between Phoenix's legs. Phoenix's hold loosened only for a moment, but Duke took full advantage of it. Phoenix saw the head-butt coming but could do nothing about it. The blow smashed into his nose and he staggered backward.

Something snapped Phoenix's head left to right, but the blood from his nose made it impossible to tell what. Phoenix felt metal against his back. Looking over his shoulder he saw nothing but darkness. Utter darkness. The light from the truck highlighted something much worse than Duke.

Moving shapes.

Phoenix felt hands around his throat. They were strong. They shook with anger.

"I...am...surprised...you can reach...my throat," Phoenix between gasps.

"You dumb worm breeder. You haven't realised the most important thing, have you?" asked Duke.

"And...what's that?" said Phoenix.

"Who do you think is driving?"

Shit!

"Now!" Duke screamed, jumping out of the way.

The pistol in the driver's hand was steady. He fired. He didn't miss.

As the slug from the bolt pistol hit Phoenix, his mind went blank, and he toppled out of the moving truck.

47

L rested her back against the wall and sank her head into her hands. How had it come to this? The constant fighting for survival. The constant struggle just to keep ahead of the sands of time. She'd thought if she left this planet she would leave all that behind.

All the fear. All the panic. All the pain.

But she had simply left one struggle and replaced it with another.

"You know, I never thought it would be like this," said L.

"How did you think it would be?" Kai asked.

"I don't know. I just thought I was leaving home for something better. Something...something... For the love of Soul–something *more*."

"Pain and struggle is part of the universe. One can't simply be without it. That is what it means to be alive."

"Really? And here was I thinking it was to have fun. To enjoy life and all its pleasures." L let out a sigh and rested her head against the cool wall. She heard movement in the darkness and felt a hand rest on her arm.

"The universe is the universe. Just allow its colours to wash over you. Be one with it," said Kai.

"Be one with it, huh? You're such a hippie." L giggled.

Nothing moved apart from their hearts. L closed her hand and allowed the warmth from her brother to flow through her. How long had they been apart? She couldn't even remember. All she knew was that it had been too long. Too many days and nights without hearing his whimsical ramblings.

"Why did you leave?" Kai asked.

"You know why."

"I guess I do. The village and its beliefs, right?"

"That, and I wanted to see more. Wanted to do more. Wanted to *be* more."

"Little L, always looking up at the stars at night. Always tinkering with machines. Always looking for answers among nuts and bolts. Everyone knew it was only a matter of time before you left. You were always a big worm in a small patch of sand. And I was always the tick just looking to catch a ride--"

"Don't call yourself that!" said L.

"But it's true." Kai let out a chuckle and patted her arm. "If it weren't for me, you wouldn't be here. I know that. And I am sorry. I know... I know... Sometimes I get lost in my work. Sometimes days pass in a blink of an eye when I'm connected--"

"It's the same for me when I'm working on a machine I can't fix."

"But I want you to know that I did try. I did try, when I found out what happened to you. I tried to dig for the truth, but Duke stopped my every advance. The lies he told were easier to believe than thinking I had failed you. Thinking that... What is buried in the dark always comes to light," said Kai.

L let out a sigh and silence once again filled the room. She patted Kai on the arm. "Well, no point dwelling on that. It won't get us anywhere."

"Have you tried looking for a way out?"

"Nah, thought I'd just sit here and wait to be rescued. What do you take me for? Of course I've tried to find a way out. But your boss--"

"He's not my boss," snapped Kai.

"Duke isn't as stupid as he looks. This room is sealed better than my toolbox, and you know what security measures I have on that."

"I never knew why. It's just a stupid old box."

"The point is we're not getting out of here anytime soon. Not unless someone breaks us out," said L.

"Then we shall be here till the stars die and Soul reclaims me again as one of hers."

L let out a snort and shook her head. "I'm not planning on being here *that* long. You can stay here and rot, but my crewmates will come and get me."

"Will they?"

"Yes. Why do you ask?"

"Because... Because not everything is as it seems, sometimes. You know, sis, sometimes people break their promises or leave friends behind. It's life. It used to get me down, but now I just accept the colour of people's hearts. It's just the way things are," Kai said in a whisper.

"Who has been filling your head with that worm shit? This isn't the Kai I knew before I went away. This isn't the brother who fought five village boys off to protect me. You have lost so much hope. You have lost so much faith.

"My crew–my *friends*–will come for me. They will tear

this city apart until I'm found. Midnight–oh, you must meet Midnight, she is the scariest person I have ever met. She is this tough, mean, fearsome Noctis female that I once saw beat up someone with their own arm. Their own arm!" L said, waving her hands in the air even though Kai couldn't see her in the darkness.

"She...sounds like fun."

"Then there is Phoenix. He's kind of the captain, but not really. Midnight lets him think that he's in charge. Well, no...I take that back. He is *my* captain. He promised me that he would look after me, and so far he has."

"Great job he's done of that," Kai snorted.

"You haven't seen the colour of his heart, Kai. If there's a way to get me out of here, Phoenix will find it. He always seems to know what to do. Then there's Plowstow... He's... He's...green."

"Just green?"

"And finally--"

The sound of a lock being pulled back drew their attention towards the door. The door hissed as it was pulled away from the walls and light grew in between the gaps it made. It was so bright it blinded the pair, who had to cover their eyes. They had become used to the dark. Used to the stillness of that pitch-black room.

As the door swung open the only visible thing was a tall humanoid outline. Light appeared to be radiating from its back, obscuring its features. It stood tall. It stood still.

A head moved from side to side and surveyed the scene in front of it. "I hope you're not planning to dally here all day, young lady. Like the great poet VVG once said, we have work to do. So do we must!"

"And, finally, there's Freyan.

48

Phoenix saw the pistol. He heard the sound. He felt the pain pass through the top corner of his chest as he tipped out the back of the hover truck. It wasn't a plasma pistol that the driver fired. It was a bolt-action hand-gun. Just his luck.

The bolt passed through his combat gear, only designed to stop light plasma fire, and ripped flesh and tore muscle as it made its way through his body.

It hurt like hell.

He fell from the back of the truck, and the ten-foot drop to the sand seemed to take forever. When was he going to hit the ground? When was he going to meet his maker?

A flash of silver blinked in and out of existence in the corner of his eye. What could that be? Phoenix reached for it and felt his hands wrap around cold steel. It felt solid. It felt reassuring. Then the kiss of sand came up to meet him in the face. Phoenix wanted to lie where he was and wait for death to greet him. His wound hurt so much. He was more tired than he'd realised.

But none of that mattered. His arm jerked ahead of him and he was pulled forward.

What the...?

He closed his mouth as his body bumped along the ground, to stop sand and other bits of debris making his mouth their home. Phoenix lifted his head up and saw that his arm was entangled in a long length of cable attached to the hover truck. He was being pulled along at speed, but if he held on, he would survive.

Nobody had noticed him yet. They all thought he was dead. He wished he were.

Phoenix looked up at the task before him and gave himself a mental slap. *Get your shit together! Come on!*

He wrapped his arm around the cable to secure a better purchase and began to pull himself forward, inch by inch. He needed to get to his feet. It sounded ridiculous, even to him, but he needed to surf the sand and save his friends. He kept dragging himself forward, hoping–and praying–that nobody from the truck made sure the job was finished.

Then again, with the black gear he wore and the darkness of the desert, he doubted if anyone could actually see him. It wasn't a theory he wanted to put to the test, though. It would be better to get back onto the truck before anyone noticed.

His wound burned as he pulled himself forward, inch by inch. Every inch was a victory. Every inch felt like a mountain climbed.

His hand slipped on the metal, and he moved back a foot or two. *Forward, fool, not backwards. Forward.*

The only thing in Phoenix's favour was the combat gear he wore. He had questioned Saoirse's choice of attire, but now he couldn't be more thankful. Anything other than the tough material would have been torn to strips by now. His face felt bruised and bloody, but it would be a lot worse if he had been bare-faced.

Phoenix lifted his head up once and saw that he still had some way to go.

"Phoenix?" Saoirse's voice spoke in his ear.

"Yup."

"I dispatched my pursuers."

Of course she had.

"Plowstow appears to be having problems, but I believe he can save himself. He...appears to have a knack for survival. What's your situation?"

"Errr, kind of busy, not--" Phoenix paused to spit out sand. "Dying. I'm making my way towards Duke via some cable."

"Are you injured?"

"Just a small hole through the chest. I should live...I hope."

"Do you need assistance?"

"Nah, I should be fine. This is a piece of cake. I just need to climb up this cable, without being seen or shot, and somehow kill two armed assholes with my bare hands. So, like I said, it should be a piece of cake."

"I am not familiar with this cake you speak of."

"It's an--"

"Earth saying," Saoirse said in a monotone voice.

"Yes, it's an Earth saying. I'm from Earth, hence I say things from there. I really don't have time to deal with this, right now. I have asses to kick."

"Are you sure you don't need help?" said Saoirse.

"I'm sure."

"Is that just your male pride and ego speaking?"

"It's.... What?"

"I shall be on my way," said Saoirse, cutting the conversation short and returning silence to Phoenix's ear.

If you were going to come, why bother asking me?

Phoenix let out a sigh of frustration and focused on the task at hand. Gripping the steel cable firmly, he pulled himself up hand over hand. He knew he would only get one chance at this. He knew that if he failed, there would be no turning back. It would be game over.

He stopped within four metres of the truck. The hover engine masked any sounds he made. Its deep bass hum echoed through his chest, keeping rhythm with his heartbeat.

Adjusting his grip on the cable, he spun his legs around so they were in front of him. Arching his back, he bent forward slightly at the waist. The cold desert air tore at his face. Riding on his butt, he took a deep breath. He began to get his feet under his knees, which were clamped together, and pulled himself into a sitting position.

Twelve months ago, if anyone had told him he would be sand skiing on a distant desert planet, Phoenix would have laughed in their face. If they had told him he would also be risking his life to get back in a hover truck he had been thrown out of, and that he would be doing so unarmed, he would have taken a swing at them.

Duke hadn't turned the hover truck around. He hadn't made sure that his prey was dead. He had left it up to fate. Well, Phoenix was going to show him and his driver that fate was indeed a cruel mistress.

49

There was one thing Phoenix had refused to address, despite its glaring at him in the forefront of his brain. One thing he was waiting for. He knew that the worms were out there. He had seen more than one moving alongside the truck.

But none had attacked him.

That in itself was more worrying than anything else.

Where were the worms?

Phoenix kept his head down and tightened his grip as the truck pulled him along. Movement to his left made him snap his head in that direction. He peered into the darkness and felt foolish for even doing so. What was he expecting to see? He felt something tickle his leg, almost making him lose his balance. Gripping the cable to steady himself, he shook his head, trying to clear his thoughts.

Shouts up ahead brought his attention back to the truck. Had they seen him? No. Shots would be coming his way. Had they seen...something else? He couldn't hear what was being said, as only a few words floated their way to him.

Easy! Relax, relax. First, stay alive. Second, make your way towards the truck. Third...well, shit. The third seemed so far away that Phoenix couldn't even think that far ahead. Trying to control his breathing, he felt the slow trickle of blood making its way down his chest. Another problem for another time.

"Phoenix! Phoenix, Phoenix, guess who?"

Once again Phoenix had to keep control of his balance as a voice boomed through his ear. "Hello, L."

"Did you miss me?"

"Hmm... Let me think on that... Hmm. Did...I...miss you? Hmm."

"Phoenix!"

"Yes, all right, I missed you, loudmouth. It's good to hear you back to your old self. Are you okay?" Phoenix whispered.

"I'm feeling so good I could dance. Actually, I have been thinking about a new one I can show you. It involves--"

"L, I am kind of busy, right now."

"Doing what?"

"What I do best."

"Fine! Just so you know, everyone is okay, and we're making our way towards the ship. Once you get to the city we'll pick you up," said L.

"Good. One question, before you go. There were a lot of small dust worms about, but now there aren't. That's a good thing, right?"

L's silence told him all he needed to know. He was in trouble. He could sense it. He could feel it. How much trouble he was in was all he wanted to know. He would have to face it head on, no matter what, and deal with it.

"Phoenix, get to the city as quick as you can. Do you hear me? Get to the city now!" said L.

"Why?"

"An alpha is coming."

"How bad?"

"Bad."

"All right, L, thanks for letting me know. Well, see you back at the city."

"Be safe."

An alpha? Logic dictated that the alpha of any species was always the biggest and strongest. Phoenix had a real problem on his hands. He had seen how big those creatures got; he had nearly been eaten by one. It was an experience that he didn't want to relive again.

But first he had to deal with the issue of Duke.

The roar of an engine sounded behind him. Argh! More problems that he could do without. He didn't have a pistol or any weapon of any sort to deal with the matter at hand. He could hear the roar of the engine getting closer and closer.

He was a sitting duck. A deer in the headlights to be picked off at leisure.

Think, Phoenix! Think!

There was nothing he could do. There was nowhere he could go. He just had to await his fate and hope that he remained hidden.

The engine got closer. Phoenix's heart pounded against his chest. His whole body grew tense, awaiting the pain that would no doubt herald his discovery.

He heard shouts up above on the hover truck. They must have also heard the engine approaching from behind. Phoenix knew that his cover would be blown–either from the front or back.

"Get ready!"

"What?"

"Are you hard of hearing?" Saoirse asked.

"No," Phoenix said in confusion.

"Then get ready! I'm coming. Prepare yourself, Phoenix Jones," said Saoirse

"Prepare myself for what?"

The war cry Saoirse screamed in his ear enveloped him whole. It was all he could hear or think about. It was like nothing Phoenix had heard of before. It was one part beautiful, two parts eerie. Its beauty was like witnessing a thunderstorm in the ocean with nothing but a raft to keep you afloat.

Phoenix felt a hand on his back as Saoirse raced past him. She picked him up and threw him forward. Phoenix was lifted clear off his feet and was airborne, heading straight for the truck. Only one thought raced through his mind.

Damn, she's strong. She held back, last time we fought.

Phoenix flew forward and saw Duke's astounded face loom into view. It was something that would keep him warm at night.

"Guess who, motherfucker!" Phoenix yelled, connecting a punch to Duke's jaw.

50

They landed in a heap, with Phoenix on top of Duke. The pistol Duke tried to raise to shoot Phoenix out of the sky clattered to the floor. Phoenix didn't waste any time; he knew what he had to do, and he needed to do it fast. He held Duke down by the throat and punched him in the face repeatedly. The wet sounds of his fist smashing into flesh echoed in the night.

Duke shoved his hands into Phoenix's face, where he dug one of his thumbs into Phoenix's eye. As Phoenix yelled in pain, his hand going to his eye, Duke used the moment to roll Phoenix off him. They rose to their feet as one, staring at each other with a mixture of emotions.

Duke was wide-eyed; a man he thought he had killed stood, large as life, in front of him.

"What's the matter, Dukey? You miss me?"

Menace touched Duke's lips; he said nothing but dived for the pistol on the floor. Phoenix threw a kick to his head. It missed but grazed Duke's shoulder, knocking him back.

Phoenix went for the pistol himself, fingers grasping at the weapon. He didn't have time to bring it up, as Duke launched himself towards him. They collapsed once again on the floor, both struggling and clawing for the pistol. They rolled around in the tight space, trying to gain the upper hand.

Duke was on top of Phoenix, pushing the pistol towards Phoenix's face. Phoenix pushed it away with every ounce of strength he had. His muscles strained; he could see Duke's finger making its way towards the trigger. Duke squeezed it just as Phoenix moved out of the way. The bolt blasted a hole through the bed of the truck, inches from Phoenix's face. He could smell the burning metal, the acrid scent threatening to bring bile up in his throat.

Phoenix bucked Duke off him, and the pistol went off once more. Phoenix didn't see where the shot went as they both struggled for the weapon. Phoenix cocked his head back and delivered a head butt to Duke's face. Duke's already bloody nose took the brunt of the force, shifting to the left, where it stayed misshapen.

Duke staggered backwards, holding his nose in his hands. Dropping his bloody hands from his face, he looked up to see Phoenix pointing the pistol in his direction.

"I guess this is how it ends," said Duke.

"It never began, Dukey. It never began."

"You won't leave this planet alive, you know. No matter what you think. No matter what you do." Duke laughed.

"Is that--"

The truck jerked to the left, knocking Phoenix and Duke off their feet. The pistol went over the side, and Phoenix watched as it disappeared into the darkness. Turning his head back, he looked towards the driver to see him slumped against the controls, a dark patch spreading across his back.

That's where the other bolt went.

Phoenix sprang to his feet but was thrown back down

once more. The out-of-control truck swerved left and right. Phoenix looked up from his hands and knees to see Duke crawling towards the controls. Phoenix tried to follow him but was hit from behind by the now free-swinging arm of the gun turret.

Stars danced in front of Phoenix's eyes.

Phoenix was launched into the air as the hover truck hit something with a bang. His arms flailed and legs kicked as he came down with a crash. Whatever the truck had hit must have been big. Or whatever had hit it.

The truck tilted on its side as it hit something again. Phoenix found himself flung forward, the impact against the side of the truck rattling his teeth in his mouth. Duke twisted the half moon steering controls, panicking as he tried to wrestle the truck back under control. But whatever the truck had hit must have damaged its controls, as no amount of turning brought the beast under control.

Phoenix found himself slammed against the side of the truck once more, and his gaze fell onto an enormous shape moving in the sand.

Shit. Is that...what hit us?

"Phoenix! You need to get off that craft before that thing attacks again," Saoirse said in his ear.

"Don't you think I know that? Saying it is much easier than doing it!"

The black-diamond body slammed itself against the truck with another resounding bang. The truck groaned under the impact. Phoenix ducked as the gun turret swung for his head. Another couple of knocks from that worm and they would flip over.

"Saoirse, what's your position?"

"Look behind you."

Phoenix turned to see a hover bike speeding towards

them. Saoirse did her best to control the bike as sand kicked up all around her. Inching the bike closer, she crept along the side of the truck.

"How do you expect me to get out the truck?" Phoenix asked.

"Jump."

"Jump where?" Phoenix asked in a panicked voice.

"Towards me," Saoirse said, holding out her hand.

"Are you out of your mind?"

"Do not fear. I will catch you."

"I'm not scared! Who said anything about being scared? I just have a healthy attachment to all my limbs, and I believe they feel the same way about me. If--"

"Stop stalling!" said Saoirse.

Phoenix let out a sigh and took in a deep breath. *Let's go, champ!* Phoenix threw one leg over the side of the truck and steadied himself as Saoirse drew in closer. He could feel his heart pounding in his chest as the truck shuddered underneath him. Breathing out slowly, he swept his gaze towards Duke, who still wrestled with the controls.

Phoenix looked ahead of him and saw Saoirse's outstretched hand. The space between them might as well have been the pits of hell. She offered sanctuary. She offered life.

A black tail erupted from the sand like Lucifer himself. It smacked the bike, knocking it sideways. Saoirse tried to right the handlebars so the bike pointed straight, but Phoenix knew without a shadow of a doubt that it was a lost cause.

"Saoirse, your hand!"

Phoenix threw half his body over the side of the truck and made a grab for Saoirse's hand. He felt her iron grip close around his hand as he caught hold of her. His muscles strained with the effort of keeping her from falling into the darkness. Phoenix felt like he was going to tear in half; one hand gripped the truck and his body bridged the gap to where Saoirse was suspended from the other.

He needed to throw her inside. He yelled in frustration, anger, and effort, tossing her back inside the truck. He lay in a heap on the floor, his heart threatening to explode, his body covered in sweat.

Phoenix looked at his hands in awe. What he had just done... It should have been impossible. It didn't make sense. He didn't have the strength–nor the speed. But... Witnessing the earlier events in slow motion...and now this... Something was definitely going on. And he knew who would give him answers to his questions.

"You okay?" Phoenix asked, looking over at Saoirse.

She panted like an Olympic sprinter. She looked across at Phoenix and nodded slowly.

Phoenix's gaze lingered on her wild eyes, dazzled with excitement, and moved down to her lips, parted as she sucked in oxygen. They kept moving down to the lines of her throat, so sleek and elegant. His gaze continued all way down to her parted jacket that showed-

"We should get moving," said Saoirse.

"Huh?"

"We should get moving. Staying here means certain death."

"I think being on here is now our only option," Phoenix said. He looked towards the cockpit and noticed it was empty. Where had Duke gone?

Shit.

He wanted to pay that fucker back for everything that he had put L through, but it seemed the little weasel had abandoned ship. Phoenix saw a hover bike speed off into the distance with two people on it. That was a problem he would have to deal with later. They had other things to worry about.

"Can you drive this thing?" Phoenix asked.

"I can operate most vehicles. This one seems simple enough."

"Good--"

Phoenix pulled Saoirse down as a hover truck sped past them, firing at the pair. Plasma flashes and bolts zipped over their heads as they ducked for cover. The light display they offered reminded Phoenix of fireflies on a summer night. The truck sped past, continuing on its journey towards the lights of the city.

"Drive," Phoenix said, moving towards the back of the truck. He manned the gun turret and looked down at the buttons in front of him. Numbers and odd shapes. Buttons he wasn't sure of. Should he touch them or not? They taunted him.

"Err.."

"Problem?" Saoirse shouted over her shoulder.

"Well, not a problem per se. More of a misunderstanding of technology."

"What?"

"I don't know what any of these mean! What do I push for it to go boom-boom?"

"There should be a handle in front of you; use that to move the turret. Next to it is a big red button. Press that to fire. Simple!"

"Easy for you to say," Phoenix mumbled.

He moved the turret, trying to lock onto the vehicle way out in front of them.

"Keep her steady!"

"Would you like to drive? Seeing as you mastered the gun controls so easily," said Saoirse.

Phoenix began to respond but swallowed his reply. He squinted through the sights once more. He wanted to make this shot count. He took a deep breath, and his hand began to descend towards the red button.

That was when the sand exploded and a monstrous head sailed up through the air, swallowing the hover truck in front of them whole.

51

L walked behind Freyan, whose senses they were using to avoid the enemy. He told L he had sneaked in and avoided guard after guard because he could pinpoint where each one was. Once he was in the building, finding L and Kai had been only a matter of time.

"You could have at least knocked out a few guards, so our task wasn't so hard," said L.

"I am a Bloodless pacifist. I can't harm, only heal and cure," said Freyan.

"I am a man of Soul, my sand brother. But I still want payback. Revenge. My hands itch for it," Kai said.

L told him, "Kai, I say this with all love, but when the fighting starts I think it's best if you don't get involved. Fighting was never your strong point."

Freyan held his hand out for everyone to stop. Turning his head left to right, he didn't make a sound. Closing one eye, he studied something that neither Kai nor L could see.

"What are you doing?" asked L.

"I have placed micro-cameras around this building. It allows me to see while remaining hidden. It appears the few guards stationed around this building are not the most vigilant. That works in our favour. But still something troubles me," said Freyan.

"What should trouble you, is that you're so white you literally glow in the dark. How are we ever going to manage to escape when you shine like a desert beacon?" L asked.

Freyan stopped in his tracks and turned his head to look back at her. She couldn't decipher his expression. "That is not what troubles me."

"Well, it should."

"No. What troubles me is that I have not seen the mercenary known as Rustem. I would assume that he would be stationed here," said Freyan.

"My capture was just a ploy to get Phoenix to act. He doesn't want me or Kai. He wants Phoenix's head. That's why we must get to my ship, so we can save everyone. Once we are safely on board, everything will be all right," L said.

"How can you be so sure? One ship doesn't change the outcome of anything. One ship is just that. One ship."

"Freyan, Freyan, Freyan," L said, patting the Bloodless on the shoulder with each word. "It is more than a ship. It is *so much more.* It is my masterpiece. It is my joy. It will change everything."

"Shit!"

There was nowhere to go. There was no way to escape. The monstrous scaled body encompassed their whole view. They couldn't avoid it. They couldn't swerve around it. It seemed as unmovable as the ground they hovered above.

Shit. Shit. Shit.

They were going to hit it. They were going to crash into it, and there was nothing they could do.

Phoenix watched the massive black body approach in slow motion. He looked all the way up towards the head and saw the horror that was its mouth. The wide circle had acted like a vacuum and simply sucked the other hover truck in. Large barbels hung down on either side of its head, moving of their own accord. No eyes. No nose. Just a body and a mouth. The ultimate killing machine.

It was beautiful, in a way; awe-inspiring.

Phoenix let out a sigh and looked up towards the stars. Distant lights winked at him with the mischievous allure of adventures yet to be had. People yet to see and women yet to please. Creatures like the dust worm that would boggle his mind. Places where diamonds were as common as sand.

He would miss all of that if he died here. All that would be missed if he didn't figure out a way to survive.

When has life been anything other than always surviving? When has it ever been easy?

Phoenix felt the sides of his lips twitch. Would he have it any other way?

Something nudged his consciousness. What was that noise?

Phoenix saw Saoirse yelling something at him. It came to him muffled, slowed, like a tape player with dying batteries. Why was she in such a panic? What was the urgency?

Oh. They were about to hit the giant dust worm and die.

That would panic anyone.

"Pho... Phoen... Phoeni... Phoenix!"

Phoenix once again felt what he could only describe as cold water trickling from the back of his brain down to his spine. As it did, the events around him came rushing back into focus.

"Stay on course!"

"But we will hit--"

"Just do it!"

"Phoenix, we'll hit that thing!"

"Saoirse. Do you trust me?"

"No!" Saoirse said with a shake of the head and a wide-eyed stare.

Phoenix tipped back his head and bellowed in laughter. "Then I need you to start! Stay on course. Full speed ahead, beautiful--"

"Don't call me--"

"Don't change course. Keep her steady!"

Saoirse looked over her shoulder at him, lips pressed thin, eyes screwed almost shut. She gave him a single nod then turned back to the controls.

Phoenix hoped this would work. He hoped that his foolhardiness would pay off.

Shit. What other choice do I have?

His finger hovered over the fire button, waiting until they were close enough. He waited until he knew the worm wouldn't be able to turn.

His mouth was dry, his palms sweaty. His heart echoed a beat. Once. Twice. He held his breath until there was no escape for the worm–or them. This had to work. It had to.

"Argh!" Phoenix slammed his finger down and held it pinned to the dashboard. The gun turret kicked and bucked backwards with the force of the shells it expelled. The blinding flashes emitting from it looked like dying stars in the darkness. Again and again, shells were vomited from the barrel and launched straight and true towards the worm's dark flesh.

Phoenix tried to keep his aim as true as could be. He looked on in grim determination as the shells began to punch a hole through the creature. Each shell helped blast the pathway for them a little wider, a little deeper.

A shriek that made Phoenix's blood run cold erupted from the worm and echoed over the sands.

They were closing in on their target. The hole Phoenix had created didn't appear to go all the way through.

They had to make it.

Phoenix brought his eye to the sight and adjusted. He fired again.

As they approached the black hole he had created, he swallowed. He couldn't see the other side. And the creature was collapsing back down.

Into the valley we go!

"Keep her steady," Phoenix screamed.

He kept his finger pressed against the fire button as they entered into darkness. He couldn't tell if they were moving or not. He couldn't tell if they were alive or not.

As the hover truck moved through the worm, like a boat through the rivers of Hades, Phoenix held his breath.

Then they were out.

Starlight from above greeted them like lost friends. As they erupted from the body of the worm, Phoenix eased his finger off the button and breathed a sigh of relief.

Phoenix looked around at his surroundings, disgusted at the sight. Lumps of worm meat covered the interior of the truck, coating it with slime. He pulled a piece from his shoulder and pulled a face as it left white strings of slime behind. He dropped it to the floor where it slapped wetly against the metal.

"What did I tell you, eh?" Phoenix said, smiling at Saoirse.

The look she gave him pinned his soul to the wall.

"Are we not alive?" he asked.

Saoirse said nothing as she wiped slime off her face.

"I saw an opportunity and I took it, Saoirse. That's what all great leaders do. A thank you wouldn't go amiss."

Her nostrils flared. She turned around with a flick of her hair and made a beeline for the city lights.

52

Phoenix surveyed the city gates as they approached. They were wide open–blasted open by some sort of weapon used to gain entry.

That's not good.

A noise to Phoenix's left drew his attention to an approaching bike. He turned the gun turret towards it but saw a green hand wave his way in panic.

Phoenix kept the gun aimed at the approaching bike. A grin split his face and he fired at the bike, aiming so the shot went wide, and heard a yell of fear ring out in the desert air.

"Hey! Hey! It's me. It's me, Phoenix. What the shit? Y'all blind?" Plowstow yelled.

"Plowstow, is that you?" Phoenix said, trying to hold back his laughter.

"Who the fuck do you think it is?" Plowstow said, now riding beside them.

"Well, you never--"

"I ain't heard a peep out of none of you! No one holo-comed old Plowstow to see how he's doing, no one came to my rescue when I was outnumbered fifty to one. I bet I didn't even cross your mind."

"Fifty to one," Phoenix said with a raised eyebrow.

"You don't believe me? Ask that she-demon you got with you. I saw her riding the opposite way when I was asking for help."

Saoirse held her head high, nose in the air, and didn't turn round to speak to Plowstow. "If you can't handle *two to one odds* then maybe this crew isn't for you."

"Two to one?" Phoenix said, his eyebrow still raised.

"Err... Well, you know... Err... With so much action going on, plasma bolts flying back and forth and the like, you can see how folk can get confused. And...and..." Plowstow allowed the sentence to die in his throat as his orange plaits flapped in the wind.

Phoenix turned his gaze back towards the city. All was silent. All appeared peaceful. But he knew what they said about appearances.

"Keep an eye out for any movement on the top of the walls."

Saoirse and Plowstow both nodded. An eerie calm rolled out from the city. The silence spoke volumes of what was about to come.

As they closed the distance, the ball of tension in Phoenix's stomach grew. No shots had been fired but he knew that something wasn't right.

"Right. We've taken out most of Duke's men but not all. Plus we still have Rustem to deal with. Everyone stay sharp. Everyone be prepared," said Phoenix.

"The destination?" Saoirse asked.

Phoenix once again looked up towards the approaching walls and clicked his tongue against the roof of his mouth. "No matter what we do, we must first take care of Duke and

Rustem. The only place we're sure to find them is at that warehouse."

"Phoenix, I'm all up for revenge and all, but ain't it easier to just skip town and run?" Plowstow asked.

"Do you always want to be looking over your shoulder? Are you okay with always wondering when the next shot or knife in the back will be coming? Do you really want to live a life like that?"

"That's the only life I know," Plowstow whispered.

"Then maybe it's time for a change." Phoenix cast his gaze sideways at Plowstow and wondered if the Orcian would turn tail and run. It didn't really matter at this point; no matter what happened, Phoenix was in it till the end.

All was quiet as they made their way through the city gates. Nothing stirred. Nothing moved.

Phoenix's gaze darted back and forth but he couldn't see their enemies. He knew they were about. He could feel it in the itch he got at the base of his skull.

These fuckers are going to make it hard on me.

The city streets were empty of all life as they hovered forward. Metal shutters protected shop window after shop window. The floating light orbs were all switched off, casting long shadows for itchy trigger fingers. Even the souls who called the alleyways their home seemed to have all disappeared.

Wind kicked up sand from the main street and blew it their way.

"Where is everyone?" Plowstow asked.

That was when the shots started to descend from the heavens.

53

"Take cover!" Phoenix didn't know where the shots were coming from. He ducked low inside the truck as blast after blast hit the side. "Saoirse, get us the hell out of here!"

Phoenix was launched backwards as the truck sped forward. Plowstow darted ahead of them, riding through back alleys and taking corners too sharply. Phoenix ducked once again as a plasma bolt hit inches from his foot.

Left. Rooftop. Ducking behind a chimney-looking structure.

Phoenix spun the gun turret around and sighted the target. Firing a shell towards his attacker, Phoenix smiled as most of the roof was blown up. Rubble rained down on the street below.

A plasma bolt from his right scorched the dashboard near his hand. Swinging the turret towards the oncoming shots he saw a face peek out from behind a window.

Phoenix aimed, fired, and the window was no more.

Saoirse took a corner hard, tilting the truck almost on its

side. Phoenix felt thuds under the vehicle that shook it. Black smoke began to billow from the back.

"Do you want the good news or the bad news?" Phoenix asked.

"Does it matter?" Saoirse shouted over her shoulder.

"Well, the good news is we're harder to see. The bad news is we're trailing black smoke, and I don't think this baby can take much more."

"We are nearly--" Saoirse cried out in pain, clutching her arm close to her body.

"Saoirse! You all right?"

"Fine," Saoirse ground out through gritted teeth.

Phoenix wanted to ask if she was sure but thought better of it. He knew it would only distract her and piss her off. He needed to clear a path towards their goal. Turning the turret from left to right, he unleashed a hailstorm of return fire. The barrel bucked and kicked out its revenge, and Phoenix aimed for anything that appeared to be a threat. The barrel glowed red hot and the smoke pouring out made it look like a cigarette on a cold winter's night.

He held his fire for a moment and scanned the rooftops and alleyways for hidden threats. There didn't appear to be any but Phoenix wasn't to be fooled so easily.

"How you holding up?"

"I told you I was fine, didn't I?" said Saoirse.

Phoenix bit back his reply. She still clutched her arm closely to her side. Gun blasts sounded off in the distance. Plowstow had run into some trouble.

Movement to his right had Phoenix swinging the turret towards his foe but there was none to be found.

Huh? I could have sworn...

Phoenix shook his head and kept his eyes peeled. They

took corner after corner; metal scraping on brickwork sent sparks flying into the air.

Another plasma bolt smashed into the side of the truck, but the attacker was gone before Phoenix could return fire. He could see the warehouse in the distance. They were getting close.

"Nearly there!"

Saoirse simply grunted. Her focus was directed straight ahead of her. Every turn could prove costly or every house a trap.

They made one final turn and their destination was in front of them. Saoirse put her foot down, and they raced towards the warehouse. But something didn't feel right. There were no guards stationed to greet them, no foes to shoot them down. They passed the guard tower unchecked, and the tension in Phoenix's stomach grew.

The huge double doors that formed the entrance to the building showed the path to freedom. Beyond it was L's ship and a way off this sand bowl.

Something up ahead caught his attention. It shimmered in the air, and Rustem appeared before them as if popping out of thin air.

"Shielding cloak!" said Saoirse.

But that wasn't what panicked Phoenix most. Rustem lifted a long tube up onto his shoulder with a flick of his hand, and Phoenix knew that it meant trouble.

"Saoirse! Stop! Stop--"

It was too late. Rustem fired his weapon and a missile snaked towards them, leaving a trail of smoke behind it. Phoenix saw it in slow motion and began to move. He had to reach Saoirse in time.

The missile headed towards him. All thoughts vanished from Phoenix's mind; he knew what he had to do. The single focus of saving his crewmate dominated his thoughts. It didn't allow room for anything else.

Phoenix raced from the back of the truck to the front. He felt like his limbs were in liquid. He urged them forward. His muscle fibres screamed in protest, but he ignored them. If he didn't move fast enough, the temporary pain he was now feeling would be over forever.

The missile was almost upon them.

Saoirse's hair flowed gently in the wind, waiting to be stroked, waiting to be touched. He was almost there; he just had to reach that bit further.

Phoenix willed his arm to grow longer as he stretched it out. *Come on, Phoenix!* He grabbed a hold of whatever he could and launched both of them sideways with all the force he had, right off the truck.

The missile struck the truck with a deafening boom, and Phoenix was blinded by a flash of light.

54

The truck exploded into a fiery ball, flipping like a tossed coin. It landed upside down, with purple, indigo and pink flames licking its body. Phoenix felt the heat from the explosion as it blasted him clear of the wreckage.

Where is Saoirse?

He couldn't feel her presence. He remembered grabbing her before the explosion, but the bits after that were too hazy to piece together.

Did she make it out okay?

Phoenix grunted as he felt his body impact something solid. He bounced once, twice, then began to roll.

What the... Oh, the ground.

Phoenix rolled along with such speed that once again he was thankful for his clothing. He came to a gradual stop and lay face down in the dirt. His ribs hurt. His back moaned. His legs refused to listen.

He groaned and tried to get up. He managed to lift himself to his hands and knees before collapsing back in the dirt. He let out a small sigh and dug his fingers into the dirt until he could feel it under his nails.

You have an opponent to face. Get. The fuck. Up.

Phoenix rose to his feet unsteadily and scanned the area for Saoirse. He found her sitting on the ground with blood trickling down the side of her face. Her eyes appeared unfocused and her hands trembled slightly. Phoenix made his way towards her, crouching low. He went to touch her chin, but his fingers never reached their destination, as Saoirse's hands grabbed his with the quickness of a pit viper. Her grip was like iron, as she slowly lifted her head up and looked him in the eye.

"Do you know how close I have come to death in my lifetime?" said Saoirse.

"No," Phoenix whispered.

"Not once. I have faced many threats, many challenges, many enemies in combat. But tonight was the first time I have ever been so close to death. If my teacher saw me now, she would be disgusted. All the trials I went through, back home, for what?

"All the pain I had to endure–for what? I allowed emotion to cloud my vision to the dangers ahead of me, to things I could have avoided. Because of that, I am in the dirt. It shall not happen again."

"It happens."

"Not to me," Saoirse said with fire in her eyes.

Phoenix heard movement behind them and lifted his head. Men were making their way towards them. He looked back to Saoirse, who had already picked herself up off the ground. He got to his feet and took a step back from her.

The bloodlust radiating off her chilled Phoenix to the bone.

Saoirse reached behind her and pulled out what

appeared to be a small pistol. She pressed a pulsing green button on its side and it began to extend outwards, growing larger and larger. A weapon that appeared every inch the assault rifle rested in her hands. Its jet-black handle ended in a hand guard Phoenix had seen on many a rapier.

"I'll handle it," said Saoirse.

"You sur--"

The look she shot his way gave him all the answers he needed.

She didn't look his way as she walked past him. "Finish this." She took aim and began to pick off the men, one by one.

It was efficient. It was ruthless. It held nothing back.

Phoenix lowered his gaze to the ground as the screams of the dying filled the air. He could tell now why she was called the demon pirate hunter. Keeping his gaze fixed on the dirt in front of him, he breathed in and out.

He lowered himself to his knees and picked up a handful of dirt. Rubbing it between his hands, he allowed the rest to fall to the ground.

Phoenix looked up towards the warehouse, to where Rustem was still standing. He hadn't moved. His arms were crossed over his chest. He appeared to be waiting for something.

I'm never one to keep people waiting.

Phoenix walked towards the Bell Man. He felt...nothing.

It surprised Phoenix; he expected to feel something. Anything. But searching inside himself, no emotions sprung forth. No anger. No hate. Nothing.

All he wanted was to save his new friends and make it out of this alive. Anything else was just a bonus. This was just part of the risks of being him.

Phoenix laughed aloud at his ego and shook his head.

"I am glad to see you approach death with a laugh and a smile. So many I have encountered have always met death with such fear. Such hate and loathing. But death is something to be celebrated. Death is something that should be loved.

"We can only start afresh because of death. We only survive because of death. We only grow because of death. So why fear it?" said Rustem.

"Did I say I feared it?" said Phoenix.

Rustem smiled Phoenix's way but said nothing.

"So you're doing good work, is that it? The work of the gods?" said Phoenix.

"Oh, no," Rustem said with a laugh. "Whatever gave you that idea? I do this for simple profit. Nothing more, nothing less. I like the finer things in life, but the finer things cost. I must do what I can do to make ends meet."

"So is that where I come in?"

"I'm afraid so," said Rustem.

"Hmm. For as long as I can remember I have always had a price on my head, or someone has always wanted something from me. Seems no matter where you go, you can never shake old problems."

"Before we start, I must say that this isn't personal--"

Phoenix threw a straight right that rocked Rustem's head back. He followed up with a kick to Rustem's solar plexus that knocked the wind from his stomach. Phoenix stepped back and looked at the mercenary with disgust.

"You capture my friends! You endanger their lives to get to me, and you say it isn't personal? You sack of shit. Where I come from, we would disagree. Now I am going to show you what we do to such people."

55

Rustem wiped blood from his nose and shook his head. "If you choose to take it that way, then I can't stop you. But know this: that will be the last time you land a blow on me."

"I've heard that before," Phoenix said with a smile.

Rustem shook his head, as if he had spoken to a child who didn't understand how grave a situation they were in. He rolled his head back and forth on his neck before repeating the motion with his shoulders. He began to walk towards Phoenix with the air of someone going for a Sunday stroll.

Phoenix threw a left and right, but both were dodged with the slightest of head movements. He threw a kick but that too was blocked.

Rustem kept on walking, backing Phoenix up further and further. Whatever Phoenix threw was blocked or simply dodged. He would always brush pass his target within a hair's breadth, but never landing one of his blows. Sweat poured into his eyes, and he could feel fatigue start to set in.

"How long will you keep this up?" Rustem asked.

"As long as I have to."

"Shall I be merciful and end it now? Or prolong your agony?"

Phoenix gritted his teeth and ran towards Rustem, but he found himself looking up at the sky as he landed on his back with a thud. Rustem had hip-tossed him as if he were a child. It took no strength or effort; it was as simple as breathing for him.

"You choose mercy, then?" said Rustem.

Phoenix rolled out of the way as a foot came down towards his face. He swayed as he climbed to his feet. It had been a long night.

Phoenix rushed Rustem once again, going high. He feinted the shot and went in low, tackling him to the ground. The look of surprise on Rustem's face was a thing of beauty, and Phoenix quickly went to work on it with his elbows. The first three blows landed, opening a cut on Rustem's forehead. The fourth missed as Rustem hip-bumped Phoenix off him.

Phoenix threw a smile at Rustem as they jumped up again. "I thought you said I wouldn't land another blow?"

Rustem said nothing as blood slowly dripped down his face. The mask he wore was a bloody one, but it showed no emotion whatsoever. That surprised Phoenix more than anything; he had thought he would be able to goad the mercenary into doing something stupid.

"Interesting," Rustem said before kicking Phoenix in the ribs.

The kick dropped Phoenix to his knees. He looked up in time to avoid the first punch thrown his way, but the others that followed found their mark.

Phoenix's head snapped back repeatedly, and he tried to stay on his feet as he swayed back and forth. His vision was blurry. He couldn't tell his right from his left. Trying to tell where the blows were coming from was proving next to impossible, as there appeared to be three Rustems standing before him.

"Interesting," said Rustem.

"Would you be so kind as to tell me--" Phoenix spat the blood that had pooled in his mouth before he continued. "What is so damn interesting?"

"Well, you have managed to land a blow against me–that, in itself, is interesting. But what really confuses me is how someone from a backward planet like yours managed to obtain nanobots. That could be the only explanation of how you have fared so well in this fight," said Rustem.

"Or maybe I'm just a better fighter than you."

"Absurd."

"Well, we do think highly of ourselves, don't we?" said Phoenix.

Rustem shook his head, the air ringing with the sound of his bells. He came at Phoenix relentlessly, showing no mercy or compassion. Phoenix was his next meal ticket; he was going to do everything in his power to try and punch it.

Phoenix could see something coming his way in the distance, which was just as well, as he wouldn't have heard what was coming towards him.

"So, Rustem, why do they call you the Bell Man?"

Rustem gave Phoenix a look as if he had asked the stupidest question in the galaxy and pointed to his hair.

"Ahh, I see. But why wear bells? A man in your line of work...doesn't that make things harder?" Phoenix asked.

"I wear them for the challenge they bring. For the simple

pleasure of knowing that it makes my work harder. I want to obtain so many things that wealth brings, but I found that if I didn't face challenges in getting them, it left me empty. So these bells make my life harder, and in doing so they make my life better."

"Rustem, you're full of shit. Have fun in the afterlife!" Phoenix said and threw himself to the ground.

Phoenix had seen Plowstow making his way towards them on the hover bike. The image was blurry, but he was certain of what he saw. As Rustem droned on, Plowstow had made his way ever closer, until he had Rustem in his sights. Plowstow pointed his pistol at the mercenary's back and opened fire.

Phoenix wasn't prepared for what happened next. The plasma blasts should have hit. They should have found their mark in Rustem's back. But Rustem side-stepped out of the way, allowing them to sail past him. He turned around and caught Plowstow by the neck, slamming him to the ground.

The driverless hover bike continued its journey and crashed into the warehouse wall. Phoenix watched in awe as Rustem held down all seven foot plus of Plowstow by his throat. The strength he displayed was mind-boggling.

So this is the true power of the nanobots.

Rustem turned his head towards Phoenix and held his gaze. He reached for Plowstow's pistol, as if he had all the time in the world.

Phoenix knew what was going to happen, but he couldn't do anything about it. His heart raced in his chest. His lungs threatened to burst because he refused to breathe. Phoenix started to get up, but he knew he would be too late. Rustem had already gripped the pistol, his fingers encircling the handle in a firm grip.

No one was going to die on this trip, he had promised himself that. Not even Plowstow. But that promise seemed to be for naught, as Rustem held the pistol over Plowstow's stomach and fired.

The scream that erupted from Plowstow's lips chilled Phoenix to the bone.

56

L made her way towards her ship.

It sparkled amidst the rust and the old metal that surrounded it. A sharp nose gave way to two flared wings attached to a long sleek body. A cluster of thrusters at the tail hinted at its speed. Red and black paintwork gave it a menacing look.

L made her way around it, slowly inspecting it. She traced a finger along the bodywork and lifted it to her face with a scowl. "Look how dirty they let you get, baby." She walked around the ship three more times before coming to a stop at the cargo bay.

"I must say, I am most impressed by this ship," Freyan said. "When you told me you built it, I was expecting some sort of tub that would just about get us out of orbit. But this looks promising. Although I am not too sure if we will ever be able to get away with those." He pointed to the missile turrets decorating each wing alongside a pair of ion cannons.

"You call those toys firepower? The good stuff is hidden away. You ain't seen nothing yet," L said with a smile.

She reached up towards the cargo hold on her tiptoes and stroked the metal panel with her fingertips. Glowing lights appeared along the cargo bay doors and the doors began to lower with a hiss. L nodded her head and began to make her way up the ramp.

Freyan began to follow her but stopped when he noticed piles of black ash on the ground. "Has your ship malfunctioned in some way?" he asked, pointing to the ash pile.

L looked over her shoulder and shook her head. "That's what you become if you try to forcibly gain entry into this baby."

Lights came on overhead with each step further inside they took. The corridor walls gleamed, with holocom screens inserted every seven metres.

"Right!" L said, clasping her hands together and turning round to face Kai and Freyan. "Welcome aboard the PHI. Onboard you will find sleeping quarters to house ten. The canteen is down the hall and to the left. I installed a machine that will cater to everyone's needs."

"DNA molecule reader built into a food dispenser?" Freyan asked.

"Only the best. I should know, I built it. Escape pods are down the corridor and each takes two. There are also escape pods in the cargo bay. If you boys would like to follow me, I'll show you to the bridge." L spun on her heel and walked away.

Freyan and Kai looked at each other before shaking their heads and going after her.

The bridge in question had everything a crew could need.

"L, how could you... This ship can rival anything I have ever flown in, and I have flown in quite a few ships. How did this come about? Like the great poet S.T. Welham once said,

'Beauty and elegance such as this is not simply made, it is won'."

L smirked, jumping up and down in joy. "It's amazing, isn't it? Truly amazing."

"Yes, but how did you do all this?" Freyan asked.

"I drew the designs myself. From the first time the idea of this ship came into my mind, I knew that it had to be made. But for that to happen, I needed a backer. That's where Duke came in. I allowed him to think this ship was his, but that was never the case. Yes, he may have paid for the resources–manpower, tools, weapons. But I oversaw all the building. Everything you see here came from this," L said, pointing to her head. "Kai built the computer system, so I know that she is one of a kind--"

Red lights flashed as sirens blared across the ship, cutting L off. "Oh... That's not right," she said.

57

The primal scream that erupted from Plowstow's mouth shook Phoenix to the core. Plowstow writhed in agony on the ground, his eyes screwed shut against the pain. Plowstow's scream quieted to a whimper as he held his stomach, huddled in a ball on the ground.

Phoenix stood stock still as Rustem slowly got to his feet. They stared at each other, neither saying a word. Phoenix couldn't hear anything even if he wanted to; a faint buzzing dominated his thoughts, drowning everything out. His mind was blank. His thoughts were nonexistent.

He could see Rustem's lips moving, but the words didn't reach his ears. It didn't really matter what was said now, anyway. None of it did. Whatever Plowstow had or hadn't done, he still didn't deserve to be treated the way Rustem treated him. He was still part of Phoenix's crew. He was still Phoenix's responsibility.

Phoenix walked towards Rustem without lowering his gaze. He didn't hesitate.

Rustem saw him coming and folded his arms over his chest, shaking his head. It was the action of a teacher who had taught a lesson repeatedly but the student still failed to get it.

Rustem's arms were still folded when Phoenix punched him in the face. The look of smugness was overridden by shock as Phoenix continued to snap the mercenary's head back with each blow he struck.

Punch, kick, head-butt, punch, kick, elbow.

Phoenix aimed at and struck any body part that he could. His blows were executed with a viciousness that he had thought long forgotten. But here it was, resurfacing like the Creature from the Black Lagoon.

Phoenix's breath was heavy and his hands bloody. He looked towards his swaying opponent.

"Well, well, Mr Jones. You are full of surprises today, aren't you? It seems those nanobots have taken to you more than I thought they had. I would love to know who your manufacturer was, just so I can--"

A shot rang out loud and clear, silencing Rustem. The man looked down at his chest as a wet patch began to spread across it. He patted it with his palm, and it came away red.

"Oh," Rustem said, turning his head to look behind him.

Duke stood with a bolt pistol raised, its smoking barrel pointing into the night sky. His arm was steady. His gaze swept over Rustem with contempt.

"You think you can fucking double-cross me? You think I wouldn't notice?" Duke said.

"I do not know what you are talking about," Rustem said.

"We had a fucking deal! I should have known that you would have taken the girl! I should have known," Duke said.

"The girl should still be--" Rustem's head snapped to Phoenix, who had a knowing smile plastered on his face. "You–" was all he got out before Phoenix punched him in the throat, dropping him to the ground.

Phoenix stepped over Rustem as if he were trash. He let his foot hang in the air above Rustem for a split second before bringing his boot crushing down on the mercenary's head. Giving his boot a final twist, he continued on his way towards Duke.

"Stay right where you are," Duke said.

"Duke, it's over. You've lost. Now, we can either do this the easy way or the hard way.'

"The easy way or...are you stupid? Do you not see who is holding the weapon? This will only end one way–with your crew's surrender. When that happens, I may allow you off this planet, if I feel like it."

"Duke, your men are dead–or soon will be. I know for a fact that you don't have L or Kai. The ship you wanted so much will soon be mine. So I will say again, you have lost. Let's stop this needless violence while we can," Phoenix said, holding his hands held out.

Duke threw back his head and let out a snort of laughter. He shook his head and looked at Phoenix with eyes that made him take a step back.

"Do you think I got to where I am by making peace? When will you fools get it? There is only one thing people respect in this universe, and that's violence. Violence and power. You can't have one without the other. So I will say it again: tell your crew to surrender."

Phoenix felt a presence by his side. Saoirse stood with her lips pressed into a fine lie.

"What do you think about his offer, Saoirse?" Phoenix asked.

Saoirse's hands moved in a blur as she flicked two knives towards Duke. One knocked the pistol from his hand, while the other embedded itself into his chest. Duke looked down at the offending knife and seemed lost for words.

"That's your answer, I guess."

58

Duke collapsed to the ground and lay there moaning, clutching the knife embedded in his chest.

"I couldn't have given a better answer myself," Phoenix. He walked over to Plowstow and knelt beside the Orcian, laying a hand on his forehead. "You still with us, big guy?"

Plowstow looked up at Phoenix and gave a slight nod. He still held his hands over his stomach wound, trying to hold back the flow of blood. Phoenix could see that there had been a lot of blood loss, and if Plowstow wasn't treated soon he would die.

"It's okay, Plowstow. Freyan will get you up and running in no time. Just hang in there for me, okay?"

"Phoenix, I don't think--"

"Don't give me that shit! Look, I promise you that you will make it, okay? Look at me. Look at me! You will make it. I know things haven't been the best between you and the crew, but that will change. I will make sure of it. I will always remember what you did for me here today. You saved my life. You gave me another chance.

"So when I say that you will make it, you will make it. Now, what are you going to do?"

"Make it," Plowstow whispered.

Phoenix gave him a small nod before getting back up to his feet. He was battered and bruised. His bolt wound was a bloody mess. He didn't feel he could move his face properly, and his body wasn't responding to the simplest commands. He moved unsteadily towards Saoirse and laid a hand on her shoulder.

She had the odd mark of battle here and there, but apart from that she appeared unharmed.

"It's almost over," said Phoenix.

"Almost?"

"Yes, almost. We still have to take care of Holger, but that is for another day." Phoenix moved past her and made his way towards the warehouse doors. His mind was foggy; thoughts chased themselves around his brain. He was tired–couldn't his brain see that? Couldn't it feel his body's energy draining away with each step he took?

His right hand was on the latch of the warehouse door before he knew it.

How did...I get here?

Phoenix shook his head and went to open the door. Something pulled at his leg. He looked down and saw Duke grimacing up at him, one hand holding onto Phoenix's leg.

"Duke, it's over, man! Either die in peace or crawl away with whatever dignity you have left."

Duke coughed and heaved, trying to get the words out. "I told you, this isn't over. It will never be over. I have sacrificed too much to get what I have. I have given too much to just allow someone like you to have it."

"You know, Duke, people like you never get it. They never know when they have lost. They never see why they lost. Should I tell you why you're lying on the ground and I'm not?"

"Oh...please...do," Duke between fits of coughing.

"It's because you never trust anyone. You never allowed anyone in. And if you did, you've already pushed them away. I used to be like you–never trusting, always thinking about myself. Always seeing what people could do for me and never the other way round.

"But luckily I saw the error of my ways. Not all of them, but most. That is why I am standing over you while you're lying there on the ground."

Duke laughed till his chest shook. He shook his head and looked at Phoenix with a bemused smile. "Phoenix...I told you this wasn't over. But now it is." Duke lifted his other hand up in the air. The device he held blinked with a red flashing light. Squeezing a button on the side sent a click through the air that silenced everything around Phoenix.

Shit!

The explosion that ripped through the warehouse engulfed it in flames.

Phoenix was thrown from the warehouse, his body turning and spinning. His senses couldn't tell which way was up. He landed on the ground and continued to roll, the force of the blast keeping his momentum going. Over and over he went until he came to a stop in the dirt.

His vision was blurry, his view peppered with dark shadows he couldn't see past. He couldn't hear anything but a faint ringing in his ears. He tried to get up but the effort proved futile.

I'm dying.

He knew it for certain, as he knew what it felt like to sleep, to laugh, to love. Phoenix lay on the ground and brought his right hand up to his face, but all he saw was a bloody mess. *Well, at least I won't need that where I'm going.* He let his hand drop back down. He wanted to close his eyes but he saw an image above him that forced them to remain open.

Saoirse moved towards him, her hair a mess, blood leaking from multiple wounds. She swayed in front of him before collapsing to her knees. She was saying something, but the words never reached his ears. Her face was a mask of pain–the kind reserved for a loss worse than the physical. He knew that face well. It was a mask he'd worn when he found out about his parents. But why was she wearing it now?

Oh...

Phoenix focused on her lips; he could see what they formed. He could see who they mourned for. L.

L had said that her ship was located behind Duke's warehouse. That he wanted it for himself. If Duke had set explosives in his warehouse, then it was safe to assume that he had also detonated some in the junkyard. The same ship junkyard that housed L's ship. Phoenix let out a sigh and closed his eyes.

He just wanted to rest. Just for a moment. Now it seemed that he would get that chance. Feeling a hand on his face he opened his eyes and saw the vague outline of Saoirse. Tears streaked her beautiful face as she cried her heart out. Phoenix couldn't stand to watch. It just highlighted his failure even more.

Bright lights hovered over Saoirse's head, bathing everything in light. He couldn't see her features anymore, just a silhouette where she knelt over him. Phoenix felt her shake him. She was trying to tell him something, trying to convey some sort of message.

"I can't hear you, Saoirse. I can't..."

Phoenix closed his eyes, letting the white light wash over him as one thought dominated his mind: I*t's true what they say about death.*

59

Phoenix's eyes fluttered open. The image before him wasn't in focus; it was as though he were looking through a greasy window. He shook his head and felt something soft beneath it. He closed and reopened his eyes, getting a clearer image. White metal ceiling greeted him. He tried to bring his hand to his face but something restricted him from doing so.

"I think he's starting to wake," L said, her face appearing above him with a wide grin. "Phoenix!"

"L, please, not so loud. He's in a fragile state."

"Hello, sleepyhead. We thought we had lost you. It was a close thing. How are you feeling?" L asked in a whisper.

"Hmur," Phoenix replied.

"That good, huh?" L said with a smile.

"How...I don't...?" said Phoenix.

"Aww, I know, I know. You're a bit confused, but Freyan says that you can't have too much mental stimulation. So I'll explain later," L said, giving him a kiss on the forehead and turning to go.

"Please," Phoenix croaked.

L let out a small sigh and passed her hands through her hair, which was the colour of a setting sun. "Freyan, look, I can't leave him like this. Bit of conversation won't hurt."

"If you must, but keep it brief," said Freyan.

L walked closer to Phoenix and laid a hand on his shoulder. "We found the ship, no problem. After Freyan broke us out, it was only a matter of making sure she ran okay again. But while we were doing that, the bombs that Duke set about the junkyard and warehouse went off. He really thought something like that could destroy this ship. He was dumber than I thought, or he underestimated the value of what he had.

"To do any damage, he needed five times the amount of explosives he used. We all live and learn, eh? Well, maybe not him," said L with a laugh.

"You okay?" Phoenix asked.

"Phoenix, I'm more than okay. Watch me dance," L said, doing a jig on the spot.

"L!" said Freyan.

"Okay, okay. If it weren't for you, Phoenix, I wouldn't have ever found my brother. I wouldn't have gotten my ship back. I would have been trapped in Dredar till the sands of my life ran out. So, for that, I thank you, and know that I will always be in your debt." L kissed him on the cheek and walked away.

Freyan took her place, holding a syringe up to the light.

"How is everyone else? Plowstow? Saoirse?"

"Saoirse only had minor injuries. Plowstow has more lives than I can count. His little stomach wound should be healed in a day or two--"

"You should cut him some slack. He did save my life."

"Hmm."

"Try and be nice to him," Phoenix sighed.

"Being nice is a way for dumb people to hedge their bets," said Freyan, still focusing on the syringe.

"I'm glad everyone come out of this okay," said Phoenix.

"Everyone else did... You, on the other hand..." said Freyan.

"How bad is it, Doc?"

"Honestly?"

Phoenix looked up and gave Freyan a tiny nod.

"Both eardrums were completely blown. I have used a temporary fix but you will need surgery. One hand suffered significant skin, muscle and nerve damage. If I'm honest, it's pretty useless and will need to be replaced. You will need facial reconstruction–multiple fractures. Both your retinas are damaged. Most of your skin suffered burns from the blast.

"If it weren't for the combat gear, you would be dead right now."

Silence filled the room as Phoenix took the information in.

"So what you're saying is that I'm fucked up?" said Phoenix.

"Pretty much," said Freyan with a small laugh.

"What happens now?"

"Now, I put you under and begin the process of surgery. I need to fill your system with nanobots. You were lucky that you had my basic ones inside you. They tried to heal you as best they could."

"Freyan. The nanobots... I did things I never could before. Time slowed down, I became stronger, my reflexes doubled. What's happening to me?"

"I told you back at Dredar, Phoenix. My little nanobots have the power to make you a super soldier. Whenever intense emotion is involved, the effects are amplified, and those were just basic ones. When I finish with you, you will be beautiful beyond measure. You will laugh at what you thought was strength, your past reflexes will look like a child's against what you will soon have.

"You will be my most beautiful creation! Now, sleep, my friend. You shall awake a god!"

60

Plowstow walked with his head down and his shoulders hunched forward. One hand tapped the handle of his pistol. The hood pulled over his head cast a shadow over his face, which was set in a deep scowl. He looked over his shoulder for the hundredth time, side-stepping into the entrance of an abandoned building. He waited and allowed his heart rate to come back down.

Did she see me?

He counted to twenty and peered round the corner. Coast clear. He stepped out of his hiding place and continued on his journey. He had to get rid of her before she left the planet. Once out in orbit she could go anywhere, be anywhere, and that was something Plowstow couldn't risk. It would always be hanging over his head. He would never know when it would come crashing down. It would be a situation that he just wasn't in control of, one that could unravel the trust that he had gained.

The orange bob moving among the few heads in the alley took a right. Plowstow followed.

His hand encircled the handle of his pistol in a death

grip. Plowstow moved faster now his target was in sight. The smell of the alley assaulted his senses. The breath billowing out before him in the night air betrayed the heat of his body; sweat poured down his back.

Plowstow took another corner and had to duck as a kick flew towards his face. He rolled out of the way and brought his pistol to bear, but that too was kicked out of his hand.

"Plowstow, Plowstow, Plowstow. I could hear you coming a mile away, big boy. To what do I owe this pleasure?" Odessa asked.

"You double-crossed me," Plowstow snarled.

"Of course I did, stupid. What did you expect? You have done the same to others countless times. It's the business we are in. It was never personal–just business. To be honest, I thought you would have bailed at the first sign of trouble. More fool you for sticking around."

"Things are different--"

"Different?" said Odessa with a laugh. "How so?"

"They just are... I think I've found somewhere...that I would like to stick around for a while. Ain't nothing set in stone, but who knows?," said Plowstow with a shrug.

"I don't see what that has to do with me," said Odessa, picking lint off her sleeve.

"Really?"

"Look, Plowstow, let's call it quits. Let's just say that I may call on you, from time to time, to ask you for a favour. If you don't do said favour, who knows what might slip out of these pretty lips of mine? I mean, uttering the wrong thing at a local inn or spaceport, and who knows who it can get back to? I mean, gossip travels fast, big boy–more so among outlaws like us."

Plowstow shook his head and began to walk towards Odessa. His face was blank, his eyes were focused.

"Now, now, big boy. Let's not do anything that we'll regret," Odessa said, her hands held high in front of her.

"I'm sorry, Odessa, but I want a clean start. With you around, I can't do that," Plowstow whispered.

Odessa's eyes grew wide. Her face paled, and her chest rose and fell. She reached behind her and pulled out a long blade, which shone in the dark.

"That won't stop me," said Plowstow.

"Well, I had to pack in a hurry, seeing how things turned out. Tell you what, let's just call it quits. No favours. It will be like me and you never even met."

Plowstow shook his head and continued forward. Odessa lunged at him with the knife, but Plowstow jumped out of the way and kicked the blade out of her hand. As the knife clattered into the darkness, Odessa's gaze followed its path longingly. While her attention was elsewhere, Plowstow threw a punch to her stomach that doubled her over.

She gasped for breath as she tried to make her escape past him, but Plowstow caught her round the throat with both hands. Odessa clawed and scratched at Plowstow, her nails digging into his skin and leaving bloody streaks. Ignoring the pain, Plowstow squeezed harder.

Odessa threw her arms behind her, trying to reach his face, trying to grab, scratch, punch–anything.

"I need this more than you. I need to be more than I am!" said Plowstow.

The animalistic grunting that escaped Odessa's lips lowered to a softer pitch with each passing second. Plowstow could feel blood running down his arms, creating a strange sensation where warm fluid met cold air.

Odessa threw her arms behind her in a final effort and her legs jerked out in front of her, kicking empty air. She gave a final small shudder, and all went quiet as her movements ceased.

Plowstow released his hold on her neck and allowed her to slide down into the dirt. He checked her pockets but didn't find anything of interest. He got up and looked at the body for a few moments before snapping his fingers. He reached for her boots and pulled both of them off. Two small pouches dropped to the ground.

He picked them up and found credits in one, but the contents of the other stole his breath away. Precious stones slipped into his open palm. They could give him the sort of lifestyle he'd always dreamed about–well, until he blew through it all.

"Ahem," said a voice behind him.

Plowstow closed his fist and spun around. Freyan stood before him with his arms crossed.

"What?" said Plowstow.

"Is that any way to speak to someone who has saved your life twice?" said Freyan.

"Twice? I was only injured once."

"Yes, you were, but if I tell Phoenix what I saw here today, you won't be alive much longer. And even if he doesn't kill you, Saoirse will do unspeakable things to you once she finds out that Rustem only knew where we were because of you--"

"You can't prove that!"

"One of the wonderful things about a Bloodless being is the tech we carry on our person. For instance, I listened to everything that was said between you and...Odessa, was it?" Freyan said, pointing to Odessa's lifeless body. "And I recorded it for later use. Plus, I recorded a video to go along with my audio, so there's that too."

"What do you want?" Plowstow asked.

"Not much. Just a favour, here or there. Nothing compared to what your little friend over there was going to have you do, I assure you."

"What's stopping me from just destroying your metal ass?"

"Phoenix was right. You can always trust a dishonest fool to do dishonest things. I thought you would say something along those lines, so I have beamed my findings back to the ship. If I am not back within the hour, it will play through the speakers of the whole ship. Then you won't have anywhere to hide, will you?"

"It's not what it looks--"

"Plowstow, I don't care. But Phoenix is willing to give you a second chance, and as you saved his life, I guess that counts for something. Now, I suggest we head back to the ship before questions start getting asked."

Plowstow gave Freyan a small nod before walking past him.

"Ahem," said Freyan.

"What?"

"I shall take the precious stones you have slipped into your left pocket. Also the three that have found their way into your coat. You can keep the credits," said Freyan.

"That be mine!"

"No, that be *the ship's*. The price those will fetch at market will put us in fuel, medical supplies and food for some time," said Freyan with his hand out.

Plowstow dropped the stones in his hand with a scowl and began to walk off, but he was stopped by Freyan. Plowstow looked down at his wrist, which was encircled by Freyan's hand, and tried to yank it free. But the effort was futile. No matter how much Plowstow pulled, the result was always the same.

"I know what you were trying to sell," said Freyan.

"I don't--"

"I found the molecular blueprints of the Warden's drug on your person after I performed surgery on you."

Plowstow licked his lips. His eyes shifted uncomfortably. He scratched his neck with is free hand. *Is this a trap?* "Look–"

"No, my empty-headed friend, you look. Do you know what those drugs could do if they got out? Do you know how selfish it was of you to steal them? Do you? I guess you don't."

Plowstow's heart raced as he tried to decide what to do. If the crew ever found out about this, he was... It really didn't bear thinking about.

"This is what will happen. I will call upon you to do something for me when I choose. It may be in a week, a year, or longer. But when I ask, you will do it. Do I make myself clear?" said Freyan.

What choice do I have? I should have left the planet when I had the chance.

Plowstow gave Freyan a small nod and began to walk off.

"Plowstow! Back at Dredar, did you set me and Phoenix up just to get your hands on the blueprints?"

"Do you really want to know?"

The cold desert wind gave the only answer that was needed.

"I thought so," Plowstow said, walking away.

61

Phoenix awoke from his slumber and opened his eyes. The same ceiling greeting him as before. He got up off the bed and planted his feet on the floor. He shivered, looking down at his naked body, and shook his head. His mouth felt bitter; his tongue was furry. He made his way to what looked like a sink and spotted a glass of clear liquid.

He brought it to his nose and gave it a sniff. Odourless didn't mean not dangerous. He brought it up to his lips and then hesitated and placed it back down.

"It is safe to drink," Freyan said from behind him.

Phoenix nodded and knocked the liquid back, washing his mouth out with it. He spat the first mouthful out and drank the rest until nothing was left. Liquid poured down the sides of his mouth as he gulped. Slamming the glass back down, Phoenix wiped his mouth with the back of his hand.

"That's better."

"The effects you are feeling right now are normal. It will wear off in a day or two."

"Why does my mouth taste like copper?"

"I could explain it to you, but..."

"Oh, I forgot. Someone from a backwards home world like mine wouldn't understand, right?" said Phoenix.

"Something like that, dear chap," said Freyan.

"How long was I out for?"

"Thirteen days."

"That long, huh?"

"If anyone else had operated on you it would have been longer, but because of my advanced skills the time was reduced significantly."

"Freyan, how many times? Being humble is a virtue that you must work on."

"But facts are facts. I must inform you that you are the proud owner of my greatest work. You are my greatest work."

"Work?" said Phoenix confused.

"Yes, work. If you turn around and look in the mirror you shall see it."

Phoenix slowly turned and walked to the mirror Freyan pointed to. He remembered Freyan telling him what he was about to have done to him. The details were foggy now.

Phoenix took one step forward and stopped. His chest rose and fell. He cast a quick glance towards Freyan, then lowered his gaze back down to the floor. He took another step and hesitated again.

If he looked in that mirror would he recognise himself anymore? Would the twins?

Phoenix stood in front of the full-length mirror and let out a sigh of relief.

"You didn't think I would change you into some monster, did you?" Freyan asked.

Phoenix didn't respond, looking his naked form up and

down. He had put on bulk and muscle. There wasn't an ounce of fat on him. Veins popped out from his arms and stomach. Bringing his hands in front of him, he rubbed one hand against the other. His right hand didn't feel right. Phoenix looked at Freyan, holding it out before him, confused.

"I told you I had to remove your hand. I couldn't repair it. Too much damage had been done. So I replaced it with a robotic one. It will still look and feel the same to everyone else–only you will know the difference," said Freyan.

"What's it covered with?" Phoenix whispered.

"Your flesh. I skin-grafted it over the metal."

Phoenix nodded his head slowly and opened and closed his fist. He moved it around, admiring the full range of motion. Phoenix moved his fingers, faster and faster, till they became a blur.

"Oh, that's not all you can do. You can crush any known alloy apart from a special metal only found on Saoirse's home world. Your hand is also impervious to heat–well, to a certain degree. Don't try grabbing a sun. You have sensors in the fingertips that can detect poisons and DNA, and can break most coded computers."

Phoenix was stunned. He blinked back tears and the image he saw magnified in size.

"Whoa, everything looks really big," he said, panicked.

"Don't worry, that is just your retinas adjusting to you. Both were damaged, so I had to repair them. While doing so, I upgraded your eyesight. You can now see eight times better. You also have night vision that will detect most heat signatures. Oh–I almost forgot. Any written language can also be translated and read."

Phoenix backed away from the mirror in shock. The

flood of information he was receiving was too much. He didn't begrudge Freyan's help, but was he even human anymore? Backing away, he bumped against a table, spilling its contents to the floor.

"Phoenix?" Freyan was walking towards him.

"What have you done to me, Freyan? Am I even human anymore?"

"Of course you are. I understand this is a lot to take in--"

"A lot to take in? A lot... Freyan--"

"Phoenix, if I didn't do what I did, you would be dead. Or worse–you would be blind, deaf and missing a hand. Would that state have been better to live in?"

"No," said Phoenix with a sigh. Walking back towards the mirror he looked at himself more closely. "At least I have kept my good looks."

A door opening to his left brought a squeal of delight, as L ran into the room and gave Phoenix a running hug.

"L, L, you're choking me," said Phoenix.

"Phoenix, I've missed you so much! I thought... I thought, I..." L buried her face in Phoenix's neck. Her warm tears trickled down his neck.

He wrapped his arms around the tiny engineer and hugged her tightly, kissing the top of her head. "I know, I thought the same thing too. But it's fine now, I'm much better. Freyan has been looking after me, so I can't complain." Phoenix kissed the top of her head once more, allowing L to settle in his arms. "You okay?" Phoenix whispered.

"Couldn't be better," L laughed, jumping away from him. "Watch me dance."

L did a little jig on the spot, and Phoenix was tempted to join her but he realised that he was naked. Bringing his hands towards his genitals, he tried to cover up.

"I've already had a good look! Yummy, yummy," L said, biting her bottom lip and giving him a wink before she left the room.

62

Phoenix made his way down the corridor, amazed at what he saw. The ship was straight out of a sci-fi movie, not like the old relics he had travelled in before. This one took his breath away. He'd never owned a luxury car back home, but he could imagine owning his first one feeling very similar to what he felt in the pit of his stomach.

He ran his hand along the spotless wall, taking in the holocoms embedded in the walls. Lights followed him, above and below, wherever he went. A small robot rolled past him, going in the opposite direction. He rounded a corner and saw L with her arms crossed over her chest.

"Welcome aboard the PHI. On board you will find sleeping quarters enough to house ten. The canteen is down the hall and to the left. There is a machine that I installed that will cater to everyone's needs..."

L ran through a speech Phoenix was sure she had rehearsed more than once. He allowed her to finish before giving her a mile-wide grin.

"The PHI–I like it. Makes it sound mean," said Phoenix.

"I am glad you like it. A shame, though, that you're wearing so many clothes. I was getting used to the sight," said L.

"Where is everyone?" Phoenix asked, quickly trying to change the subject.

"Right this way."

L turned on her heel and led him down a few corridors. Phoenix poked his head through every door they passed, till L grabbed him by the shirt and pulled him along.

"All in good time," said L.

They came to a set of double doors and walked through to the bridge.

"Now this is what I call a bridge!" said Phoenix. He walked forward and was greeted by a viewing screen that showed him the brown sands of the desert. He looked towards L and sent a worried glance her way.

"Don't worry, we are parked on a huge rock structure; we're safe from dust worms. Don't think I would be as stupid as that," said L.

"You sure?"

"Yes, I'm sure. Now, Midnight is our pilot, and she will handle the actual flying of the ship."

Phoenix turned his head back and saw Saoirse looking at a bunch of controls that made his head hurt just looking at them.

She looked up and gave him a simple nod. "Glad to see that you are well, Phoenix. Now that you have stopped lazing about, there is--"

"Lazing about? Is that what you call what I went through? If it wasn't..." Phoenix let out a sigh and rolled his eyes. "Nice to see you too, beautiful."

Saoirse's jaw clamped together and her nostrils flared. She climbed to her feet, and L jumped between them.

"Play nice, play nice. Now, where was I? Oh yes, and Plowstow is our weapons gunner," said L.

Phoenix looked over at Plowstow, who seemed to be asleep. His head was back, his eyes closed, drool making its way out of the corner of his mouth. Phoenix walked over and slapped him on the shoulder, jolting him awake.

"What! What! What," Plowstow said, looking around guiltily. "I wasn't sleeping, I was just--"

"Plowstow, I'm glad to see you. Once again, I must thank you for risking your life for me. If it wasn't for you, I wouldn't be here today," said Phoenix, enveloping Plowstow in a tight embrace.

Plowstow allowed his arms to hang limply by his sides as Phoenix embraced him. His eyes darted all around the room, searching for the hidden danger.

"Thank you, once again," said Phoenix, pulling away.

"And finally, Kai will be dealing with our navigation. He created the computer system for the ship, so I think that it's only right," said L.

Kai's long shaggy hair hung in his eyes as he looked back at Phoenix. "By the power of Soul, I am glad to see you up and about."

"Same goes to you, Kai. Happy to have you on board. Now, where do I sit, L?"

"Right here," L said, pointing to a chair in the centre of the bridge.

"Is this..." Phoenix said, eyes wide, a small smile on his lips.

Saoirse rolled her eyes and went back to looking at the screens in front of her.

The chair in question was all black with a red stripe down the middle. It appeared to be made from some sort of leather.

If there was a space equivalent of a throne, he was looking at it. Phoenix walked around the chair, taking it in. He leaned close to L. "Is this the captain's chair?" he whispered.

"Yes. Just don't mention it or certain people will get annoyed," said L, pointing not at all subtly in Saoirse's direction.

Phoenix lowered himself into the chair and allowed it to hug his body. Placing his hands on the armrests, he noticed that there were little grooves for his fingers. They fitted perfectly.

"When did you...?" Phoenix looked at L, confused.

"I took your measurements while you were asleep. Naked," L said, waggling her eyebrow up and down.

Plowstow let out a snort but snapped his head forward when Phoenix glared his way.

Phoenix settled his body into the chair and sighed. "It's like I'm sitting on a cloud. It's wonderful, L. Thank you." Something caught his attention on the table next to him. It was a holocom, one that he didn't recognise.

"It's Rustem's. All I could find was that, but not his body," said Saoirse.

Phoenix picked it up and moved it back and forth between his hands. A small smile danced on his lips as he slotted it in his pocket. "Right, ladies and gentlemen. What do you say we take this baby into outer orbit and see what she can do?"

"Oh, great, this shall be the first time I get to see it leave orbit," said L.

"What...do you mean?" Plowstow asked.

"Well, with one thing and another, and everything that has happened, we kind of never got round to taking her off-planet. But–but..." said L as horrified faces swept her way.

"I'm pretty sure that it will be fine. What's the worst that can happen?" she said with a nervous laugh.

"What!"

"L, I don't think--"

"I ain't risking my life on hopes an' dreams. I'm too young to die!"

"Maybe if we were to test--"

"Enough!" Phoenix shouted, slamming his hand down on his armrest. "Now, L, are you sure this thing can fly safely in space?"

"Phoenix, I wouldn't be on here if I didn't think it could," said L.

"That's good enough for me," he replied.

"I'll just make my way to the engine room to make sure everything is all right. Take off when you're ready," said L, leaving the bridge.

Phoenix leaned back in his seat and closed his eyes. Another adventure awaited, but before that, he had some payback to deliver.

"Saoirse, take her up when you're ready," said Phoenix.

He felt the roar of the engines vibrate through the ship. Already he could tell that this thing was more powerful by far than anything else he had flown in.

"Any direction in mind?" Saoirse asked.

"No. Just up."

The ship rocked slightly then shot up in the blink of an eye. The force it took off with pushed Phoenix's head flat against the chair. They were pulling at speeds that boggled his mind.

"Shit!" Phoenix said, gripping the chair as the viewing screen showed clouds and then the first hints of space.

"Uh-oh," L's voice said through the ship's speakers.

"What uh-oh? No uh-oh!" Plowstow said, his voice shaking.

"We've lost the power to all the engines! I think we're going down," said L.

Silence filled the spaceship as the sound of the engines cut out. Four faces looked at each other, open-mouthed and wide-eyed.

"I'm too young to--"

Then there was a roar as the engines kicked back into life and kept on pushing them forward. L's laughter sounded eerie, sweeping through the halls of the ship via the speakers. "I'm joking! I'm joking! All is fine."

"L!" said the four, making their way off the bridge to deliver their own brand of justice.

EPILOGUE

Holger sat surrounded by bowls of half-finished meals. Stains coated the front of the shirt he wore. He wiped crumbs from his mouth with the back of his sleeve, but it did little to clean the mess on his face.

One of his servants walked in from a door to his left. Holger could feel her hovering just out of his peripheral vision.

"Yes?"

"Excuse me, my lord, but... But... Are you finished with your meal?"

"Does it look like I am still eating?" said Holger.

"No...no, my lord," said the servant.

"Then I am done then, ain't I, you dot!"

Holger leaned back in his chair and watched in silence as she bent forward and began to pick up his plates. His eyes travelled down the front of her uniform and he lifted his head.

Although her eyes were cast down, Holger could still see a slight tremble in her lips.

"Err... There is also some food that fell down on the floor in front of me–if you just make your way round to this side of the table, I am sure you can find it," said Holger.

"I will wait till you are done with the room, my lord. That way I can clean it better without disturbing you."

"It can't wait. I shall be using this room for some time, and the odour is affecting my concentration," said Holger.

"I really think--"

"I didn't ask you to think! I asked you to do!" said Holger.

The servant's lips parted–about to say something–but the wide-eyed glare from Holger made her swallow her words instead. Making her way round the table, she faced Holger, picking up what she could find.

"I think if you turn around you will be able to do a proper job."

The silence that followed that statement felt like a noose round the servant's neck. Holger watched her like a snake watching a mouse; the closer she got the quieter the room seemed to get. Now facing away from Holger, the servant bent forward at the waist and began to pick up what she could find with speed.

"What's the rush," Holger whispered, his fingers tracing up and down her thighs.

"I--"

"Shush, shush." His fingers made their way upwards, like a spider crawling up a drain, but were halted before they got to their web-caught prey.

Holger's holocom beeped, breaking the silence of the room. Was that a sigh he heard the servant make? Grunting in frustration Holger dismissed her with a wave of his hand.

"Hello?"

"Guess who, motherfucker!" said a blank screen.

"Who is this?"

"I'll give you three guesses."

"This is a secure line! Do you know who I am?"

"I have said once before, anyone that says that ain't worth much," said the voice.

"My father--"

"Should be ashamed that his DNA made you. That you are the best excuse that his DNA can come up with. Because that in itself is a blow that would crush any father," said the voice.

"How dare you!"

"You still don't wanna guess?"

"I will find you! I will kill your mother, rape your--"

"*Listen* to me, you fucker! You should have left me well alone. You had your chance–even after you put me through hell. Even after you tore me from my family, I was prepared--"

"I don't care--"

"I was prepared to let bygones be bygones. But now..." The voice paused and tutted. "I'm coming for you, Holger. I'm coming for you, Holger," sang the voice.

"I will crush you," said Holger.

Laughter came through the holocom and echoed through the room. "If Rustem couldn't do shit, what makes you think that you can?"

"You..." Holger uttered the word like a dying man's last regret.

63

REVENGE (SPACE OUTLAW 3)

Trex peered over his glasses and sighed at the screen. He took a sip from his glass and shook his head. His fingers resumed punching codes and numbers into a floating data pad in front of his face. He scowled once again at the message that the screen displayed.

Bold red letters flashed irritatingly on the screen, mocking his attempts.

He pinched the bridge of his nose, closed his eyes and let out a sigh. His fingers flew across the data pad as he tried once more, but the outcome was still the same. The red letters appeared to be bolder this time; louder in their mockery of him.

"Argh! This is getting us nowhere!" Trex shouted in frustration.

His colleagues lifted their heads from behind their screens, spread around the room. A few buried their heads deeper into the work they were trying to do. Screen shots of planets littered the walls of the room along with graphs; some with numbers scrawled across them and others with red crosses slashed through them.

"What do you expect?" asked Bill, who sat next to him.

"I didn't expect it to be this hard. I mean, the job was simple enough. The job *itself* is easy. But we can't do anything if the Council are watching our every step. He does know that, doesn't he? We weren't all blessed with a powerful father," said Trex.

"Trex!" Bill said with a glare.

"Oh, what? Don't give me that. Everyone in there is thinking the same thing. Everyone knows what a pain he can be. Everyone else is just too cowardly to say it."

Murmurs swept through the room like the rustling of leaves.

"Oh shut up! I'm still the head researcher in this facility, and if anyone so much as breathes about what is spoken in this room, I will know it has come from one of you. You think what we do here is dangerous because *the Council* may find out?" said Trex, his glare sweeping the room. "Just let me go back to Holger empty handed and i'll show you dangerous. What the Council might do will pale in comparison to what he will do to us. To our families--"

"Trex, this won't help morale--"

"I don't care if it helps morale or not. All I care about is getting results. Results will allow us to go back to our families. This planet needs to be found. I can't stall him any longer." Trex breathed out a heavy sigh as he once again, pinched the bridge of his nose. He picked up the papers sprawled across his desk and, giving them another passing glance, threw them into the air.

He turned in his chair and took in his colleagues.Each one sat in front of a screen and a data pad similar to his. Everyone who had been turned his way now ducked down behind their monitors, furrowed brows adorning every face.

Trex pushed his horn rimmed glasses back up the

bridge of his nose and found Bill still looking his way. "What?"

"Why do you bother with those ridiculous things on your face? I mean do they even have a function?" Bill asked.

"When I visited the planet known as Earth, people who were vision impaired wore them."

"That still doesn't answer my question. Plus you are not vision impaired. The surgery for corrective eyesight is hardy expensive," said Bill.

"It's something called fashion. I know the concept is a hard one for you to-"

A high pitched wail filled the room and echoed through the surrounding halls. Trex shot up from his chair, knocking it to the floor. Faces turned to him in confusion.

"That's the security alarm," said Bill.

"I know very well what it is, you incompetent halfwit. What I want to know is why it is going off. The guards aren't running another systems drill, are they?"

Bill looked at him and offered a small shrug.

"Oh, for goodness' sake! Why do I even keep you around?" Trex marched towards the holocom embedded in the wall and said, "What is the meaning of this? We are not scheduled for another security drill any time this month. This won't do! We are doing important work here! Work that must not be interrupted-"

Three explosions shook the room and knocked everyone off their feet. The overhead lights blinked out and were replaced with the dim glow of the emergency ones. Screens fell off desks and smashed on the floor.

Trex began to make his way to his feet, but he was once again knocked to the ground as another explosion shook the building. His colleagues screams of pain and fright bounced from wall to wall.

Trex stayed on his hands and knees and surveyed the room. Blood oozed from a wound on one woman's scalp. Others tried to stem the bleeding, but even from where he crouched, Trex could see that they were losing the battle.

"Shut up, all of you! This is not a drill," Trex said, crawling towards his desk on his hands and knees.

"What do you think is happening?" Bill asked.

"As you well know, Bill, I'm not psychic, so I don't know."

"Do you think it could be pirates?

"No. All the major players have been paid off, and the ones that haven't been aren't big enough to worry about. Plus they wouldn't dare--they know who this lab belongs to."

Gun shots could be heard in the distance, hinting at things to come. Screams came from outside the lab, silencing the ones inside it. No one spoke, and everyone looked at each other with wide eyed stares.

"Trex, what shall we do?" Bill asked.

"I'll tell you what we won't do--we won't panic. That's what we won't do. Keep calm, everyone. I mean, I mean... This... This. I'm sure everything is under control. I'm sure that the guards are dealing with the perpetrators as we speak. There is nothing to worry about, absolutely-"

"Trex, I don't think-"

"Didn't I tell you not to worry, Bill!" Trex's head snapped left to right, his eyes darting to the only exit in the room. "Quiet! We mustn't make a racket. Look, you see, we'll be alright, the metal shutters are coming down."

With a jerk and a start, the metal shutters sealed the only entrance and exit to the lab. It met the ground with a final slam that any casket would be proud to make. The windows were covered by metal, and the faint glow from the overhead lights cast long shadows on everyone's face.

"See, everything is going to be all right. I told you, didn't

I? I told you that all this needless worrying would get you nowhere. We have food and water capsules in here that will last us weeks--till help arrives."

A knocking came from the metal shutters. It was faint; no one would've heard it, if the tortured silence wasn't ruling inside the lab.

Heads turned and people glanced at each other in shocked silence. Trex licked his lips, pulling at the collar of his shirt.

The knocking came again; three deliberate taps.

Trex placed his fingers to his lips and crawled backwards, away from the metal shutters. His hands left wet imprints on the stone floor. His back touched a wooden desk behind him, and he yelped in surprise, bringing his hand up to smother the sound.

Three taps rang out for the third time.

"We know you're in there! Come out, come out!" sang a voice from outside of the metal shutters.

The sound came again.

Everyone held their breath inside the lab, sitting in silence, waiting for something to happen. Waiting for something to come out from the shadows.

"We know you're in there! Open up! Trust me, if you don't you're not going to like what's about to happen..."

Beating hearts pounded against chests but nobody broke the silence.

"They can't get in," mouthed Trex.

The metal shutters shook and rattled but held tight. Everyone breathed a collective sigh of relief, but it was short lived as the metal exploded inwards. Shrapnel flew in all directions, injuring the lucky and killing those closest to the shutters.

Trex held his breath until the smoke cleared and the

debris settled to the floor. Coughs could be heard all around him, and he covered his mouth with his hands.

A black male, with a bone earring in one ear, strode through the hole. He stood in the centre of the lab and cast a disappointed gaze over the scene. "All this could have been avoided," he said, waving a hand at the dead and wounded. "It's a shame it had to end this way. I would like to say you're all innocent parties in this, but we know that isn't true, don't we? We all know what you've been doing here."

A midnight blue female walked through the hole, accompanied by a green brute who was all of seven feet tall. They both folded their arms across their chests.

"Now, I will take all the data you've researched and gathered for Holger, and you'd better make it fast," said the black male.

"And why would we do that?" Trex asked.

"Because if you don't, you have...oh..." He looked at his wrist and gave a shake of his head. "Five minutes before this place blows up. And seeing as we are blocking the only way out of here, I suggest that you start gathering that data."

"No matter where you go, he will find out who you are. He will come for you," said Trex.

With a laugh that boomed through the room, the man shook his head and said, "Tell Holger that Phoenix Jones is coming for him."

AUTHOR NOTE

Want to know when the next book is out, updates, get chapters and cover reveals before anyone else. Sign up to my mailing list by clicking here. I will never spam you and only email you once a month, with news about the latest release and the like.

Now that's out of the way let's continue.

First thing's first. I want to give a shout out to the wonderful Tandy, for proofreading these books off her own back. She caught a lot of typos, that weary eyes and long nights allowed to get through. So for that, I'm thankful.

This second book, by far was one of my most enjoyable books to write. The words came quick and fast, faster than any book before really, and it had a flow that I have never had before or since. Everything went right with this book, and a lot of things that just happened in the magic of writing it.

Blake not being able to speak was just something that happened. When I first thought of him, he could speak and laugh with the best of them, but something told me to go with a different angle and I did.

We got to see a softer side to all our main characters, and I'm not too sure if that will last or not. Plowstow loves being a dick, and Freyan loves proving how much smarter he is than everyone else.

As always I want to take a moment and say thank you.

Thank you for reaching all the way to this part of the

book, thank you for taking your time in reading what I've wrote, and thank you for taking a chance on me, when I basically just write crazy stories that are on my mind.

So from the bottom of my heart, thank you.

If you could take a moment to leave a review, that would be more than welcome. k

Till next time,

Hugs and kisses.

P.S (Click here to sign up for the newsletter)

Writer@dominiquemondesir.co.uk

Printed in Great Britain
by Amazon

46647765R00162